The Yumi Trees

Matthew John wishes to go into space.
The captain of the starship does not like bats.
Will Matthew John's bat Bulmer be left behind?
Or will the bat sneak aboard?

ARTIBEUS

ANTHONY BARTON

The Yumi Trees

WITH DECORATIONS BY THE AUTHOR

Bulmer Press

THE YUMI TREES

Bulmer Press Edition
Copyright © 2011 Anthony Barton
Library and Archives Canada Cataloguing in Publication
Barton, Anthony, 1942-
The Yumi Trees / Anthony Barton.
ISBN 978-0-9869038-6-1
I. Title.
PS8553.A7776Y86 2011   jC813'.6   C2011-905434-5
Cover and drawings by Anthony Barton. All Rights Reserved.

TO THE BOYS AND GIRLS
WHO READ BAT RIDER
ADVENTURES

This book is for you.
I hope you like it.

Contents

CHAPTER I

A Birthday Present for Bulmer

BATS find it hard to open presents. They have only one clawed thumb on each wing, and this makes them clumsy. 'This is for you, Bulmer,' I say, holding up the brightly colored package. 'The label says "Happy Birthday, Bulmer! With love from Matthew John." Shall I take the paper off?'

'Yes, please,' says Bulmer, eager to see his gift.

'Here goes,' I say, and pull away the wrapping to reveal a long metal object with yellow and black stripes.

'It's a springy thingy,' says Bulmer.

'It's called a pogo stick,' I say. 'Put your feet on the pedals and then jump up and down.'

'Whoee!' says Bulmer, bouncing about in the Bat Cave on his pogo stick. 'Look at me, everybody!

Matthew John gave me a springy thingy.'

The other bats chatter loudly among themselves. They all want to try out the pogo stick.

Bulmer says they may take turns.

After they have all had a bounce or two on the stick, a velvet bat by the name of Pinky asks 'Why did Matthew John give Bulmer a pogo stick?'

'That's a long story,' I reply.

'Tell us,' says Suki, the bat from Number One Squadron.

'You all played your parts,' I say to the bats crowding around me. 'Don't you remember?'

'We do and we don't,' said Bulmer.

'Before I start,' I say, 'you should know that Matthew John grows a little bigger every day. This worries him. He fears that one day he may become too big to ride on Bulmer's back. He is fond of Bulmer and does not want to be a bat rider without a bat.'

Bulmer puts down his pogo stick and looks at me, wide-eyed.

I take a deep breath. 'This is the tale of the Yumi Trees. It begins on the day Matthew John first met the captain of the Artibeus. Do you want to hear what happened?'

'Yes, please,' say the bats.

THE YUMI TREES

CHAPTER II

How Matthew John Went Into Space

ADDISON CARTER, the captain of the Artibeus, held out his glass for more of Mr. Seeds's dandelion wine. 'Bats!' he said, and aimed a kick at Bulmer.

Bulmer hopped out of the way in a hurry, flapping his wings to keep his balance.

'Don't you treat Bulmer like that!' said Matthew John, jumping to his feet.

Addison Carter narrowed his eyes. 'If you want to

join my ship, lad, you'll leave that flea-ridden pet of yours behind.'

'Bulmer doesn't have fleas,' said Matthew John. 'At least I don't think he does, and he's not a pet.' He would have said more but Mr. Seeds put a hand on his arm.

'I'm sorry you lost Misty, Addison Carter,' said Mr. Seeds.

'I didn't lose Misty. She flew off and abandoned me, the stupid no-good bat,' said the captain, downing his wine. 'Bats can't be trusted.'

'Do you have *any* bats on board?' asked Matthew John.

'I have one bat in my ship. His name is Crystal. He's my navigator. I couldn't manage the hyperspace jumps without him,' said Addison Carter, 'but I keep him chained to the deck in the navigation wind tunnel, and I don't let him fly.'

'That's horrible,' said Matthew John.

'Crystal does jumps?' asked Bulmer, puzzled.

'And I don't let him speak, not unless he is spoken to,' said the captain, putting down his empty glass with a bang and rising to his feet. 'Well, boy, are you coming aboard? I hear the docking clamps engaging.'

'I suppose I am,' said Matthew John. 'Goodbye, Bulmer.' He gave his bat a fierce hug.

'Bye-bye,' said Bulmer. 'I'll miss you, Matthew John.'

'Thanks for coming to see me off,' said Matthew John.

The airlock doors hissed open.

'Enjoy your time in space,' said Mr. Seeds. 'Keep away from the Dinosaur Deck.'

Matthew John's mother ran a comb through his hair. 'I've put a bar of chocolate in your pocket,' she said.

His father shook his hand. 'The best of luck with your tour of duty, Matthew John.'

'Thanks, Dad. Thanks, Mum.' Out of the corner of his eye Matthew John could see his friends saying goodbye to their parents. He spun on his heel and strode down the ramp into the starship. His friends followed him. Neither he nor any of his fellow bat riders looked back at the bats they were leaving behind. They could not bear to. They were used to having their bats with them wherever they went.

The bats watched their riders depart and talked quietly among themselves.

'I wish I could go on the starship with Matthew

John,' said Bulmer.

'Me, too,' said Smoky. 'I wish I could go with Joshua Ryan.'

Hula nodded. She was going to miss her own rider, Annabelle Sue. But what could they do? Their riders had to join the ship and the ship's captain would not allow bats to go with them.

'If we did board the ship, we'd get into trouble,' said Emily Charlotte's bat Vesper.

'I wouldn't mind if we did,' said Hula. 'I like trouble.'

'Let's play Tag,' said Kiti, the young tiger cub who liked to play with the bats. She jumped on top of an empty shipping container. 'I'm It.'

Smoky made a grab for Kiti and missed.

Smoky and Kiti tumbled inside the container.

'Purp,' said Kiti. This was a good game. She could move faster than the bats, whose legs were joined to their wings. She scrambled up the inside wall of the container, using her tiny claws.

Vesper and Hula spread their wings and flew to the rim of the container to tag her.

'Purp! Purp!' said Kiti, letting go with one paw to bat at them.

'Don't worry, Kiti, I'll save you,' said Bulmer, who did not know the rules of the game. 'Here I come.'

Bulmer's sudden arrival knocked Vesper and Hula into the container. Kiti lost her grip and fell, too. Bulmer landed on top of her.

'Uh. Sorry,' said Bulmer. 'I guess I shouldn't have done that.'

The four bats and the tiger cub lay in a heap inside the container.

'Mmmph humph,' said Smoky, who was at the bottom of the heap, and found it hard to speak.

They were inside a modern programmed container. The container could understand and speak one hundred and seventeen languages, and knew that in the language of the Purple-toed Sloths of Epsilon Erandi, 'Mmmph humph' meant 'This container should go on board.'

'Goomph whoof phumph Artibeus,' the container replied in the same language. This meant 'I have activated my anti-gravity unit and I am floating through the airlock of the Artibeus.'

So that was how Kiti the tiger cub and the four bats joined the ship without anybody knowing. Neither the officers nor the men of the Artibeus saw anything unusual in a container floating into the ship.

There was a thump as the docking clamps let go. Matthew John and his friends pressed their noses to the transparent viewport and watched the shuttle float away into the darkness of space, ferrying Mr. Seeds and their parents back to the planet of the mile-high Yumi trees.

'I hope they get home safely,' said Emily Charlotte.

The first officer ran up to the captain, came to attention, and saluted. 'Sir! We have just received an urgent signal asking for our help. The signal originated in the system of Sol Niger.'

'The Black Sun?' said Addison Carter. 'That's where I lost my Misty. Start up the wind tunnel. Crystal, lay in a course!'

'Not more hyperspace! I can't stand it any more! It's driving me mad,' said Crystal the bat navigator, rattling his chain. 'Please, captain. Don't make me.'

'Stop whining, you good-for-nothing bat!' said Addison Carter. 'Warp speed!'

The Artibeus leapt for the stars.

They dropped out of warp in the Sol Niger system. Hundreds of rocky planets whizzed around a dark star that spun so fast that it made Matthew John dizzy to look at it. Countless thousands of asteroids smashed into the ship's force screens, exploding like fireworks. Matthew John, who had been given the task of watering the Yumi trees on the ship's bridge, found the ship shaking so badly that he could not hold his watering can steady. By mistake, he watered the captain's feet.

'Fool!' said Addison Carter, pushing Matthew John to one side as he strode to the navigation wind tunnel. 'What have you done this time, Crystal? Have you forgotten how to use your ears? Have you forgotten how to navigate?'

'It's the chain, sir,' said Crystal. 'I need to be free to fly so I can see where we are going in hyperspace. I can't work properly padlocked to the deck.'

'Don't you try that on me, you pitiful excuse for a bat,' said Addison Carter. 'If I free you from your chain, you'll fly away like my Misty did. I won't risk it.'

Crystal's ears pricked up. 'Something's coming, captain,' he said.

'What do you mean?' asked Addison Carter.

Crystal closed his eyes and listened to echoes in hyperspace. 'Something really big is rushing towards us.'

'Collision stations! More power to the force screens!' said Addison Carter.

'Too late, captain,' said Crystal.

Something hit the Artibeus with a big thump.

'Emergency!' said the ship's computer. 'Hull breach on the Dinosaur Deck.'

A mysterious hooded and cloaked figure appeared on the bridge, clutching a glowing stone.

'Who the devil are you?' said Addison Carter. 'What are you doing on my ship?'

'We are the Mormoops,' said the cloaked figure. 'We have come for you, captain.'

Matthew John threw his empty watering can at the cloaked figure. The watering can knocked the glowing stone from the intruder's grasp. The stone hit the deck with a flash of purple light, and rolled towards Matthew John's feet. He picked it up. The stone was a smooth crystal. It sizzled with power. Hairs rose on the back of Matthew John's hand.

'Give me back that stone!' said the cloaked figure.

'Come and get it, Mormoops,' said Matthew John,

and pressed a button on the armrest of the captain's chair. The button was labeled E-G-T.

The trap doors to the Emergency Gravity Tube hissed open, and Matthew John, his friends, and the captain dived into the tube.

'You cannot escape!' cried the cloaked figure, and dived after them.

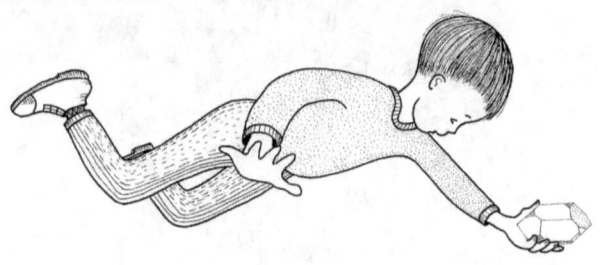

Matthew John, his friends and the captain spread their arms and legs wide as they plummeted down the gravity tube. They plunged through the lower decks of the Artibeus. White-painted signs flashed past them: CREW QUARTERS, STEERAGE, and LOADING BAYS. They flew past a sign saying ELECTRICAL ENGINEERING. Men in coveralls looked up from their work to watch them go by.

Wind ruffled Matthew John's hair. He looked over his shoulder and saw the cloaked figure swooping after them, head bent forwards and downwards like a bird of prey. The figure seemed to have two long, thin legs.

'I want that stone back!' shouted the cloaked figure.

A sign read DINOSAUR DECK.

Matthew John shouted 'Exit!'

'Deck Seventy-Two,' said the computer. 'Natural History. Late Cretaceous. Order Dinosauria.'

Matthew John and his companions landed on the tail of a plant-eating dinosaur named Bronto. They ran along Bronto's long bumpy back.

They climbed up Bronto's long neck. Panting for breath, they headed for Bronto's small head.

Soon Matthew John could hear the plant-eating dinosaur's jaws munching on the leaves of a Yumi tree.

'I have caught you!' said the cloaked figure with the long, spindly legs, swooping down out of the gravity tube, wings spread wide.

'That's what you think!' said Matthew John. 'Look over your shoulder!'

A meat-eating dinosaur burst from the ship's forest. It was as tall as a house, with a huge face and a big, gaping mouth. The monster gave a mighty roar that shook the trees, and lunged toward the cloaked figure.

The cloaked figure swerved to escape the meat-eating dinosaur, bounced off a tree trunk, and tumbled down among the bushes.

This was Matthew John's chance. He ran across the broad, flat expanse of the plant-eating dinosaur's head, and his friends and the captain followed him.

Bronto paid no attention. He was not a bright plant-eating dinosaur. He had a very small brain in his head and another very small brain near his tail. Both brains were thinking about how nice the leaves tasted. A moment ago, Bronto's eyes had been surprised to see a meat-eating dinosaur leap out of the forest, and had sent an urgent message about this to the brain near his tail. The urgent message said: 'A meat-eating dinosaur has leapt out of the forest!' Unfortunately this urgent message had to travel all the way from one end of Bronto to the other. The message had not yet arrived, and so Bronto had no idea that he was in danger, and went on happily munching away at the leaves.

Matthew John slipped the stone into his pocket for safekeeping. He reached up above his head with both hands and opened a panel in the deckhead. He hauled himself up into one of the ship's air ducts and then reached down to help his friends and his captain join him there.

The meat-eating dinosaur spotted them and thundered towards them, smashing aside trees. It was hungry.

Addison Carter was barely inside the duct when the meat-eating dinosaur shattered the panel and reached into the duct with its front legs, scrabbling about and trying to grab the bat riders. Luckily the dinosaur had only two claws on each hand.

'Run!' said Matthew John. 'Keep your heads down!'

Matthew John, his friends and the captain ran as fast as they could along the air duct. Matthew John

27

looked back to see if they were being followed, but it was too dark to be sure. The meat-eating dinosaur roared again. Matthew John felt the air duct shake. The meat-eating dinosaur was coming!

'You have a plan for retaking the ship?' asked Annabelle Sue as they ran.

'I'm thinking one up,' said Matthew John. 'What's that smell?'

'Peanut Butter Banana Wheels,' said Annabelle Sue, salivating.

'The ship's galley! Quick! Help me with this panel.'

Matthew John slid a panel aside and jumped feet first into the galley. The galley was where the meals were prepared for the officers and crew of the Artibeus. It was a huge kitchen filled with quivering desserts and wonderful aromas.

Matthew John and Annabelle Sue landed in an Almond Pie sprinkled with sugar.

Emily Charlotte and Joshua Ryan landed in a Chocolate Voodoo Bombshell.

Captain Addison Carter landed in a Tuxedo Truffle Torte.

The chef was a pot-bellied man wearing a white chef's hat. 'Vot haf you done? You have ruined my

Tarta de Santiago!' he said, rushing at Annabelle Sue and waving a wooden spoon.

'Daddy!' said Annabelle Sue. 'Stop! It's me!'

'My little cupcake!' said Chef Wandor, throwing down the spoon and giving his daughter a sticky hug. 'My Annabelle Sue! We are together again. You have dropped into the galley to see your Papa!'

'We're in trouble,' said Annabelle Sue. 'Daddy, what are you doing here on board the Artibeus?'

'Your Mamma is running the restaurant. I am here to see that nothing happens to Daddy's little girl in space. How are things going with you? What sort of trouble are you in today?'

'Oh, the usual kind,' Annabelle Sue replied. 'The ship's been taken over by a strange figure wearing a cloak and I'm being chased by a meat-eating dinosaur.'

'Never fear, my brave little strawberry tart!' said

the chef. 'If that dinosaur puts its nose into my galley, then I shall turn it into a dish fit for kings.'

'Save some for me,' said Annabelle Sue, licking the almond sugar off her fingers. 'Listen. I have to run. Right now we're really busy. Sorry we can't stay! See you! Bye!'

'A presto!' said her father, and waved goodbye as his daughter ran out of the galley with her friends and the ship's captain.

Moments later the meat-eating dinosaur came crashing through the deckhead and landed in the middle of the galley, sending Chef Wandor's pots and pans flying.

'WHERE'S... MY... PREY?' bellowed the slavering beast in a voice like thunder.

'Your prey is in here,' said Chef Wandor, and swung open the door to his largest oven.

'RRR!' roared the meat-eating dinosaur, and dashed inside the oven. The dinosaur hit the far wall of the oven and stunned itself.

Chef Wandor closed the oven door. A dreamy look came into his eyes. He kissed his fingers. 'Vol-au-vents Tyrannosaurus,' he said to himself, 'in a sauce Royale. I shall be famous. Wandor the Wonderful, they will call me. I shall be the greatest chef in the universe, and all thanks to my Annabelle Sue.'

Matthew John, his friends, and the captain ran along the Galley Deck until they came to a mass of twisted metal where an asteroid had slammed into the Artibeus, making a hole in the ship's side. An emergency force field flickered, keeping out the coldness of space.

'That asteroid looks hollow,' said Joshua Ryan.

'Hollow?' said Matthew John.

They hurried to the asteroid.

A fold of skin gaped to greet them.

'I don't think this is an asteroid at all,' said Addison Carter.

'Let's see what it looks like inside,' said Matthew John, and led the way in through the hole in the skin.

'It's beautiful,' said Emily Charlotte, gazing around her in wonder. 'Look at those lovely red veins radiating from that central hub, those crimson tendrils, and that great bell pulsing with life.'

'I can hear something,' said Annabelle Sue, and set off down a ribbed corridor to investigate. She brushed her fingers on the pink tendrils that lined the passage. The tendrils she touched shivered and withdrew a little. They were tickly.

Emily Charlotte followed close behind. 'The air feels hot and clammy,' she said.

The sound grew louder: Hoomp-diddy, hoomp-diddy.

'The floor is sloping down,' said Annabelle Sue, feeling her way forwards in the dim light. 'The slope is becoming steeper.'

'Don't fall,' said Matthew John. 'Be careful.'

'I *am* being care – ' said Annabelle Sue. 'Uh-oh! I'm sliding.'

Matthew John flung himself forward. He grabbed Annabelle Sue by the arm. 'Don't worry,' he said. 'I've got you.'

'Who's got you?' said Annabelle Sue, as she and Matthew John began to slide together down the slope, holding onto one another's arms.

'Help!' said Matthew John. 'Annabelle Sue and I are slipping into some kind of pit. Keep back, Emily

Charlotte! Don't try to help us, Joshua Ryan!'

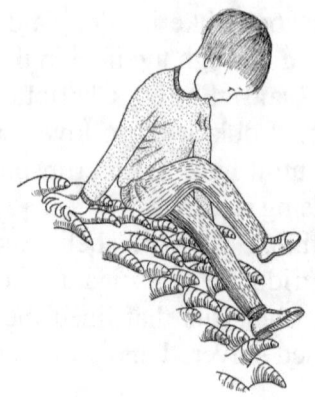

'If they won't help you, I will,' said Addison Carter, and he pushed his way forward, knocking Emily Charlotte and Joshua Ryan off balance.

All four bat riders and their captain slid helplessly down into the pit.

HOOMP-DIDDY! HOOMP-DIDDY!

Down, down, down they slid. They could not stop themselves.

HOOMP-DIDDY! HOOMP-DIDDY!

They slid to a halt at the bottom.

The sound stopped.

All was silent.

Matthew John was the first back on his feet. 'We must climb back up and out of this,' he said, and tried his best to climb out of the pit, but found that he could not. All of the tendrils that had helped him slide down now prevented him from climbing up. 'It's a trap,' he said. 'We are stuck down here.'

'I wonder where "here" is,' said Annabelle Sue, peering about her in the gloom.

As if in answer to her question, a dim red radiance filled the bottom of the pit.

'We are trapped inside a living space vessel,' said Addison Carter, staring about him in amazement. 'Look over here. This must be the control console used to fly the ship. It has two seats fixed to the deck in front of it. This must be a ship designed for two. But there is something funny about the seats.' He walked over to look more closely. He whistled. 'That's odd,' he said. 'One chair is designed for a human to sit in and the other chair is designed for a bat to hang upside down in. I wish Misty were here. She'd love to hang out in a chair like this.'

'So would Bulmer,' said Matthew John, walking over to join the captain. He ran his hands over the smooth upholstery of the bat chair. He dug into his pocket. 'Have some of my chocolate,' he said, passing bits around. 'I'm afraid the hot rock has melted it a little.'

'It tastes all right,' said Emily Charlotte. 'Thanks.'

'I'll save this last piece for Bulmer,' said Matthew John, and wrapped the morsel in its silver paper. He slipped it into his other pocket, the one that did not have the hot rock in it.

'If only we had our bats with us,' said Annabelle Sue, 'we could jump on their backs and make our escape, but you made us leave our bats behind on the shuttle, captain.'

'Bulmer, Smoky, Vesper and Hula will be missing us,' said Emily Charlotte.

'I wonder what they are doing,' said Joshua Ryan.

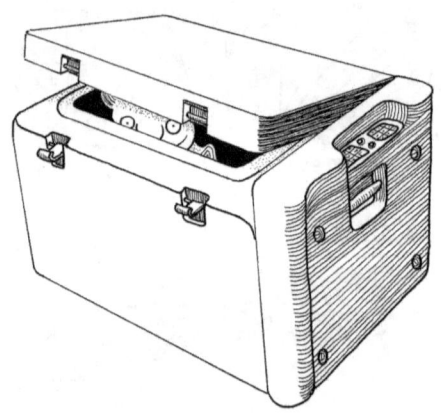

Bulmer lifted the lid of the shipping container and looked out. He saw a bunk, a basin, and mirror. 'Where are we?' he whispered.

'You are in the captain's cabin of the Artibeus,' said the container.

'Ssh!' said Bulmer. 'Not so loud. Someone might hear you!'

Unfortunately for Bulmer, in the language of the Water Spiders of Zeta Draconis, 'Ssh! Not so loud! Someone might hear you!' means 'This container has arrived at its destination and should be emptied at once.' The container was good at languages. It upended itself, sending the four bats and the tiger cub tumbling out onto the deck.

'Oo!' said Bulmer. 'That hurt!'

'Good thing the captain has a rug,' said Hula.

'At least we can breathe again,' said Smoky.

'We're not supposed to be here,' said Vesper. 'I expect we are all going to suffer.'

'Purp!' said Kiti the tiger cub, jumping up on the bunk. She attacked the captain's pillow.

She was too young to have teeth, but just wait until she did! Pillows would run away from her, squealing with fear.

The cabin door hissed open.

'Somebody's coming!' said Smoky.

Smoky, Vesper, Hula and Bulmer dived under the bunk. Kiti hid her head under the pillow.

A hooded and cloaked figure entered the cabin and wobbled precariously over to look in the mirror above the basin. 'Hear and obey us,' said the cloaked figure. 'We are the Mormoops!'

The figure adjusted its hood and moved closer to the mirror. 'Your starship belongs to me,' said the figure, talking to the mirror. 'Wo-ho-ho-ho!'

'Your voice is too squeaky,' said Hula, from under the bunk. 'You don't sound scary enough. Your Wo-ho-ho-ho has to come from the pit of your stomach, like this: WO-HO-HO-HO!'

'Who says my voice is too squeaky?' said the cloaked figure, turning away from the mirror and peering about the cabin.

The bats showed themselves. 'I am Hula, and these are my friends Smoky, Vesper and Bulmer. Who are you?'

The figure let her cloak slide to the floor and took off her hood. She was a bat, and she was balanced precariously on two long sticks of wood.

'Purp!' said Kiti, taking her head from under the pillow.

The strange bat had not expected to see a tiger cub, and wobbled, trying to keep her balance. 'We are the

Mor - OOPS!'

The strange bat toppled over and landed on her head on the rug. Her long sticks clattered to the deck.

'Tell us your real name,' said Hula.

'Misty,' said the strange bat, sitting up and rubbing her head. 'My real name is Misty.' She covered her face with her wings. 'I had a message for my bat rider, Addison Carter, but a boy took it from me. When I chased the boy to get the message back, I met a meat-eating dinosaur and tumbled into the bushes. After that I came back here to this cabin to try to work up the courage to go and tell Addison Carter who I really am. Do you think he will be angry with me?'

'No, Misty, I don't think the captain will be angry with you,' said Smoky. 'I think he'll be thrilled to see you. Take us to Addison Carter right now and we'll help you make peace with him. Can you fly?'

'Of course I can fly,' said Misty, uncovering her face and giving her wings a vigorous flap. 'I'm a bat, aren't I?'

Led by Misty, the five bats swooped down the gravity tube and into the Dinosaur Deck, where they landed on Bronto's head.

'What's this huge thingy we've landed on?' asked Bulmer.

'It is just a plant-eating dinosaur,' said Misty. 'Don't worry. It is very stupid. It won't hurt you.'

Misty did not know about the urgent message that was making its way from Bronto's eyes to his lower brain.

The message arrived. Bronto's lower brain lit up.

'A meat-eating dinosaur has been seen by the eyes,' the lower brain said to itself. 'H'm.' The lower brain thought about this news for a while and then sent a new message to the legs. This new message said 'RUN!'

Bronto's four legs weighed a hundred tons each. When they received the new message, they began pounding up and down like pistons.

'Hang on!' said Bulmer.

The five bats dug their claws into Bronto's head. Kiti the tiger cub dug her claws into Vesper.

'Ow!' said Vesper.

'Purp!' said Kiti.

Bronto galloped through the rain forest of the Dinosaur Deck. The bats clung to Bronto's head. Bronto knocked over several Yumi trees. A flock of parrots rose into the air in a panic, crying 'Bronto saw us! Bronto saw us!'

'What a ride!' said Bulmer, hanging on for dear life.

In the ship's galley, all of the great ovens and mixing bowls rattled and shook as the plant-eating dinosaur thundered overhead, but Chef Wandor was busy filling puff pastries with Tyrannosaurus savory sauce and did not even look up. He was focused entirely on putting the finishing touches to his Dish of the Day.

Bronto thundered straight out of the forest and out onto the asteroid. Bronto tripped over the fold of skin and landed with a thump on his belly with his legs stuck out in four different directions. He spun around and around and slid to a halt. This was the most exciting thing that had ever happened to him. He grinned happily.

As Bronto came to a sudden halt, the five bats and Kiti were flung over the dinosaur's head. The fold of skin yawned wide. They were catapulted inside the asteroid. They spread their wings in a hurry, circled and landed at the bottom of the pit beside the two chairs and the console.

They folded their wings and looked about them. They saw Addison Carter. They saw their bat riders.

'Matthew John!' said Bulmer.

Matthew John ruffled the fur on the top of Bulmer's head. 'It's good to see you again, Bulmer. Have some chocolate,' he said and gave his bat the piece he had saved.

'Thanks,' said Bulmer.

'How did you come aboard, Bulmer?' asked Matthew John. 'And who is this strange bat you have brought with you?'

'Her name is Misty,' whispered Bulmer.

'Joshua Ryan!' said Smoky.

'Smoky!' said Joshua Ryan. 'You've come to rescue us! Thank you!'

'You're welcome,' said Smoky.

'Annabelle Sue!' said Hula.

'About time you showed up,' said Annabelle Sue.

'Emily Charlotte,' said Vesper. 'You're not dead.'

'Sorry to disappoint you, Vesper,' said Emily Charlotte, and gave her bat a big hug.

'Addison Carter!' said Misty.

'Misty?' said Addison Carter, hardly daring to believe his eyes. 'Misty? Is that you? You unfaithful bat! You deserted me! You left me to die on an asteroid. I was lucky the Artibeus found me before my oxygen ran out.'

'I did not desert you,' said Misty. 'This is the very asteroid on which you abandoned me, and this is the very pit into which I tumbled. Why did you not find me in the pit? Why did you not rescue me?'

'I searched for you,' said Addison Carter. 'I searched and searched.' He burst into tears. 'Oh, Misty! I'm so sorry.'

Misty wrapped her wings around him. 'I forgive you,' she said.

'Where did this bat Misty spring from?' said Matthew John softly, scratching his head.

'She was the cloaked figure on the bridge,' said Smoky. 'The one you took the stone from. She was balanced on two long bits of wood to make her look tall and imposing.'

Addison Carter clasped Misty tightly. 'We're together again. That's all that matters. But why the cloak? Why the stilts? Why did you not tell me who you were? What's all this about the Mormoops? Who are the Mormoops?'

'The Mormoops are bats,' said Misty. 'They have their own planet. I had to dress up in the cloak and then chase you into this living ship so that you might hear and see hear for yourself the message from the Mormoops.'

'The Mormoops have sent us a message?' asked Addison Carter. He stopped hugging his long-lost bat, and stepped back to have a better look at her. It was wonderful to see her again. He was overjoyed. But what was she talking about? 'Where is this message?' he went on. 'I want to hear it.'

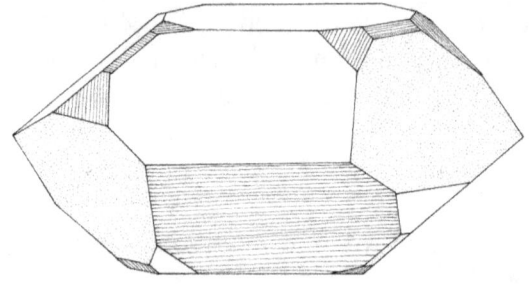

'The message is in the stone that Matthew John took from me,' said Misty.

'This?' said Matthew John, fishing the glowing stone from his pocket.

'Place the stone inside the hole in the console,' said Misty.

Matthew John looked at his captain for permission.

Addison Carter nodded. 'Go ahead,' he said. 'It's time we found out what all of this is about.'

So Matthew John slipped the stone into the hole. The stone fitted snugly inside the hole. There was a whirring sound. The stone brightened and began to broadcast the message from the Mormoops.

A faraway world took shape.

Matthew John felt as though he were floating in the air over a city of trembling spires lit by a purple sun. He heard bells pealing and felt a deep longing to swoop down into the city. Strange peeps and wild hoots were heard. An image took form, hanging in the air. It was the face of the ugliest bat Matthew John had ever seen.

The bat was black all over, with curved incisors and nostrils like gun barrels. The ugly bat had cauliflower ears. Under the ugly bat's chin hung curtains of flesh fringed with creepy-looking hairs.

The image of the ugly bat spoke. 'We are the Mormoops,' it said in a deep voice. 'Come to our planet, Misty. Freedom awaits you. No longer will you have to bear the burden of slavery. No longer will you be forced to do the bidding of your human overlords. Bring your angry bat-hating captain with you. We have built this vessel to carry the pair of you to visit us. Your journey will begin the moment you remove the message stone from the console.'

Matthew John looked up. 'Did everyone hear that?'

His friends nodded.

'I suppose I am the angry bat-hating captain,' said Addison Carter. He sighed. 'All my life I have dreamed of visiting an alien world. Here's my chance. How do you feel about it, Misty? Do you want to go?'

'Yes,' said Misty. 'I want to visit a world run by bats. Let's travel to that world together in this living ship the Mormoops have so kindly sent for us.'

'If you go to their world,' said Vesper, 'then I expect the Mormoops will eat you. They look like vampire bats to me.'

'Don't remove the stone from the console until my friends and I are safely out of here,' said Matthew John. 'What shall I tell the men, captain?'

'Tell them you are the new captain of the

Artibeus,' said Addison Carter, shaking hands with Matthew John. 'Congratulations, Captain Matthew John. The Artibeus is yours now. She's a good starship. I know you'll see her safely home.'

'I shall see her safely home,' said Matthew John, raising his chin and looking Addison Carter in the eye. 'Good luck on your voyage of discovery, Addison Carter. Good luck to you, too, Misty. Have a safe journey, both of you.' He turned to his friends. 'Mount your bats, riders! Kiti, you're with me!' He leapt onto Bulmer's back and pumped his fist. Bulmer took off.

Thrilled to be riding their bats once more, the four bat riders took off, executed a minimum radius turn, and flew through the fold of skin and out of the Mormoops vessel. They did a quick inverted tuck-over roll to avoid a pack of hunting raptors roaming the Dinosaur Deck, and then flew in echelon formation straight up the gravity tube to the bridge of the Artibeus. There they dismounted and ran over to the transparent viewport in time to see the Mormoops vessel break free. They saw Bronto the plant-eating dinosaur leap for the safety of the forest. They watched the asteroid ship head out into deep space, carrying Addison Carter and Misty away on their historic journey.

'I'm your new captain,' said Matthew John, turning to the first officer. 'Report!'

'The force fields are failing,' said the officer. 'Our only navigation bat, Crystal, has gnawed through his chain and is hiding in the bridge broom closet. He refuses to come out. The Artibeus is diving into the Black Sun. In five seconds we shall all be dead.'

'Bulmer,' said Matthew John. 'Hop into the wind tunnel and take Crystal's place. Close your eyes. See if you can see hyperspace.'

Bulmer did what he was told. He began beating his wings, flying with his nose to the wind and going nowhere. He closed his eyes and listened. 'I hear ... wiggly things,' he said.

'Grab the wiggly things with your mind. Give them a twist.'

'Like this?' said Bulmer.

The black sun vanished. The Artibeus burst into the Pleiades system, trailing clouds of dust lit by starlight.

'Woo!' said Bulmer. 'That was fun!' He gave the wiggly things a squeeze.

The Artibeus was transported to the glowing remains of a supernova.

'How lovely!' said Emily Charlotte. 'Do something else, Bulmer.'

'Uh. Okay,' said Bulmer, and turned the wiggly things inside out.

The Artibeus leapt right out of the galaxy. Billions of stars spilled out into intergalactic space.

'Cool,' said Joshua Ryan.

'All those different blues and pinks!' said Hula. 'It's like a festival of lights.'

'Does this crazy bat know how to take us home?' said Annabelle Sue, tapping her foot on the deck.

'Think of our own planet, Bulmer,' said Matthew John, 'and concentrate.'

'Like this?' asked Bulmer, who had never been a navigation bat before.

In rapid succession the Artibeus popped in and out of the Crab Nebula, Orion's Belt and the constellation of Sagittarius.

'I dink I'm going to sneeze,' said Bulmer. 'Ahhh…choo!'

As Bulmer blew his nose, the Artibeus popped into orbit above a planet covered with Yumi trees and circled by a moon close enough to fly to.

'We're home!' said Matthew John. 'It's all right, Crystal. You can come out of the broom closet now. I promise that you'll never be chained to the deck again, not for as long as I am captain.'

The broom closet door opened and Crystal hobbled out. 'Free at last!' he said, and fainted.

'Take Crystal to the sick bay,' said Matthew John to the first officer. 'See that he has a proper meal. He looks half starved.'

'Gladly, sir,' said the first officer, and took Crystal gently up into his arms and carried him away.

The shuttle met them and locked on. The airlock doors hissed open.

Bulmer switched off the wind tunnel. He wiped the sweat from his brow. 'Now I can relax,' he said, 'and enjoy some peace and quiet. I'm safe. I'm home. Nothing can harm me now.'

Kiti's mother, the huge tigress Baagh, leaped through the airlock and slammed Bulmer to the deck with one paw. 'Where is she?' she roared.

'Yodortassa-feinda-torkin-tainer,' said Bulmer. It was hard to speak with Baagh's paw pressing on his head. He was trying to tell Baagh that her daughter Kiti was safe and hiding inside the talking container.

Now in the language of the Hissing Swans of 61 Cygni, 'Yodortassa-feinda-torkin-tainer,' means 'Attack the big furry animal with the black and yellow stripes.'

Proud of its skill at languages, the container flew through the air and bonked the tigress Baagh on the head.

'BAAGH!' said Baagh, and leaped into the air. She was furious. No container had ever dared do such a thing to her before. She raised her paw and was about to strike back, when out popped Kiti.

'Surprise!' said Kiti.

'My Oodle-Ums!' said Baagh, and gave her daughter a big hug. 'I thought I'd lost you, my Inky-Pinky-Doodle. Where have you been?'

'Mummy, Mummy!' said Kiti. 'I played Tag with the bats and we were on a ship and there was person in a cloak who was really a bat, and I rode on a dinosaur.'

'I'm glad you had a good time,' said Baagh. 'But you must never go off on your own again. You had me worried half to death.'

'Me, too,' said Bulmer, struggling to his feet and

feeling himself all over to make sure he was still in one piece.

Parents came aboard. There were warm greetings from all of the bat riders.

'I do hope you did nothing to embarrass your captain,' said Matthew John's Mummy, wondering why her son's face was covered in mud and slime.

'Matthew John *is* the captain,' said Bulmer. 'He saved the ship.'

'It was really Bulmer who saved us,' said Matthew John. 'He's the best navigator in the whole galaxy. You should have seen the amazing places he took us to.'

'Well done, both of you!' said Daddy. 'I'm bursting with pride.'

'So am I,' said Mr. Seeds, wheeling his chair through the hissing doors. 'I trust you took my advice and steered clear of the Dinosaur Deck, Matthew John?'

Matthew John did not know what to say. He stared down at his muddy sneakers and blushed.

Chef Wandor came to his rescue, bearing a steaming platter of stuffed pastries. 'Have one of my vol-au-vents, Mr. Seeds.'

'Thank you,' said Mr. Seeds, and popped the pastry in his mouth. 'Delectable!' he said with his mouth full. 'You must tell me your recipe.'

'I never tell anyone my secrets,' said Chef Wandor, and winked at Annabelle Sue.

The bat riders and their parents all crowded round the platter and helped themselves to Chef Wandor's delicious pastries.

CHAPTER III

Miss Pretty Flower and the Leopard

'THERE ARE five elements,' said the teacher, Miss Pretty Flower.

'There are heaps more elements than that,' said Annabelle Sue.

'There are one hundred and eighteen elements,' said Joshua Ryan, who was good at science.

'This is a class in fortune telling, Master Joshua Ryan and Miss Annabelle Sue. In fortune telling, there are five elements,' said Miss Pretty Flower, and pursed her lips.

'My bat Vesper can tell fortunes,' said Emily Charlotte. 'She's always predicting that gloomy things are going to happen.'

'My bat Bulmer can bend time and space,' said Matthew John, not wanting to be left out. 'He says the future is all wiggly.' He looked over his shoulder to see if Bulmer was at the back of the classroom, where the bats liked to hang out. 'I don't see our bats,' he said and frowned. 'Where have they gone?'

'I have sent all of your bats to the Bat Cave for a special class in navigation,' said Miss Pretty Flower. 'Now pay attention, everyone. The names of the five elements are Earth, Fire, Wind, Water and Space.' She turned her back on her pupils and wrote the names of the five elements on the board. She then faced the class to tell the boys and girls what she wanted them to do. 'Write the five names in your exercise books, please. Did anyone forget to bring a pencil?'

'I leant mine to Pinky,' said a boy in the back row.

'You may use my pencil, Master Gabriel Logan,' said the teacher, and offered it to him.

'Thanks, Miss Pretty Flower,' said Gabriel Logan. He borrowed her pencil and, copying from the board, wrote the names of the five fortune-telling elements in his book in his neatest handwriting.

Matthew John bent over his own book. He had just finished writing the word 'Space' when his Bat Rider phone trembled in his pocket. He put his hand up. 'Permission to leave the room?' he asked.

'Of course, Master Matthew John,' said Miss

Pretty Flower, giving the boy a look that meant 'Don't be long!'

Matthew John jumped to his feet, opened a sliding door made of rice paper, and stepped outside onto the verandah. He slid the rice paper door back to close it behind him. He breathed in the fresh air and looked down on the ocean that stretched away to the horizon. The school was perched halfway up the side of the hill. It was a good place to study in peace. They had the whole island of Kanji to themselves. A flock of bush-warblers rose from the trees, crying out in alarm.

'Yes?' he said, answering his phone.

'Artibeus here, captain,' said the voice of his first officer. 'Sensors have detected a giant ocean wave rushing towards you. The science officer says you have ten minutes before the wave reaches your island. I'm sorry to say we can't help you. We're still stuck up here in orbit repairing damage done to the ship by the Mormoops.'

'Thank you, first officer,' said Matthew John. He pushed the red Bat Alert button on his phone that linked him directly to his nearest squadron of bat riders, which was Number One Squadron. 'Akihito Akemi?' he said. 'Is that you? This is your group captain speaking. We have an emergency. Scramble all your riders and fly as fast as you can to the school on the island of Kanji. Your mission is to save the children from a giant wave.'

'I strike temple bell to summon bat riders,' said Akihito Akemi. 'We come to save you, Matthew John.'

Matthew John replaced his Bat Rider phone in his pocket. He slid the rice paper wall open and stepped inside the classroom. He walked up to the front of the class. 'I'm sorry to be a nuisance, Miss Pretty Flower,' he said, 'but a huge wave is coming and we have to evacuate the school. Bat riders are on their way to rescue us.'

Miss Pretty Flower pressed her palms together and bowed to the class. 'Fire drill!' she said. 'Everybody line up by the door!'

During the din of chairs being pushed back, Matthew John said quietly 'Miss Pretty Flower, you are too big to ride on the back of a bat. We shan't be able to fly you off the island. How will you escape from so big a wave?'

'Do not worry about me, Master Matthew John,' said Miss Pretty Flower, straightening her kimono, which was red. 'Just make sure that you and all the other children are safe. That is what matters.'

Akihito Akemi sounded the temple bell in the Hall of a Hundred Bats. He tightened his obi belt, and dashed across the narrow wooden bridge that arched over the lotus pond. Hard on his heels came the other ninety-nine bat riders of Number One Squadron. All were smartly dressed in their bat riding uniforms. They ran into the Pine Chamber and whistled for their bats. Akihito's bat Suki was the first to swoop down from the pagoda roof. She did a backward flip and gripped the steam-powered launching trapeze with her feet.

'Ho!' cried Akihito Akemi. 'You are quickest bat in squadron, Suki!' He somersaulted onto Suki's back, jerked the lanyard that released the steam, and felt the rush of cold air as he and his bat were catapulted out of the open window and into the sky. Ninety-nine other bat riders were catapulted after him, and the air filled with steam.

'Head for Kanji Island,' he said into his bat rider phone. 'Great wave coming. Rescue schoolchildren. Fly fast, fly high, my samurai!'

'We hear you, Akihito Akemi,' his ninety-nine fellow bat riders answered in unison.

Akihito Akemi patted his bat's neck and said softly 'Give it all you've got, Suki. We must be in Kanji before wave hits island.'

'Hold on tight please, honorable master,' said Suki. She put her head down and raced through the clouds of the gathering storm, her wings beating as fast as a humming bird.

'Eep! Eep!' she cried, and cocked her hooded ears to hear the sound of her own voice rebounding. She could not yet sense any echo of the island, nor of the wave, but she could sense the echoes of the ninety-nine other bats and riders flying behind her. They were in a tight V-formation. The whole of Number One Squadron was in the air, and she was right out in front, leading the way. We rush to the rescue, she thought. I hope we shall be in time.

Hyou, the leopard of Kanji, padded to the entrance to his lair and sniffed the air. Something was up. The bush-warblers were behaving strangely. A great many mice were fleeing up the hill.

He put a paw on top of one of them.

'What are you running away from, little mouse?' growled Hyou.

'Big wet thing coming,' squeaked the mouse.

'H'm,' said Hyou, and lifted his paw.

The mouse scampered on up the slope.

Hyou furrowed his brow. He was a mighty leopard. He was supposed to be able to figure things out. One mouse plus another mouse equals how many mice? Hyou shook his head. He had no head for numbers. Letters bothered him, too. He knew there were letters called A, B and C. He had heard that if you put the letters together they made a word. He tried putting A, B and C together, but nothing happened. No word came into his mind. He felt sad. He was a mighty leopard, but he was mightily uneducated.

He longed to go to school. He could see the school on the slope below his lair. The school had a red tiled roof that curled up at the corners, and a garden of boulders surrounded by raked gravel. Hyou had tried creeping up on the school once, but the children had seen him coming and had screamed. That was the trouble with being a leopard. When people see you coming, they do not think 'Here is a leopard who wants to learn to read, write and do sums.' They think 'Here is a leopard who wants to eat us,' and then they scream.

Hyou lowered his body until his belly was touching the ground. His tail moved restlessly. He peered between the grass stalks. He watched the children pour out of the school and head up the hill. He saw their teacher, Miss Pretty Flower, walking with them. His heart beat faster in his chest. Miss Pretty Flower and her pupils were coming to see him!

He became excited. This had never happened before. He had never before seen the whole school, teacher and children, come marching up the hill. Miss Pretty Flower must have heard of his thirst for knowledge. She must be hurrying up the hill to help him make his dream come true. Soon she would teach him to sing 'Now I know my ABC.' He was thrilled.

'I won't have to go to the school after all,' thought Hyou. 'The school is coming to me.'

Hyou broke cover. He stood out in the open and said his own name loudly so that the schoolchildren and Miss Pretty Flower would know where to find him. 'Hyou!' he roared. 'Hyou!'

As he gave voice, the sky darkened.

Hyou looked out to sea. There was a change in the weather. The mouse had been right. Something big and wet was coming, and it was coming soon.

The erupting volcano Mount Boom had shaken the rocks under the sea. The shaking rocks had made a giant wave. It was the kind of wave that surfers dream about. It was huge and green and smooth, and, as it approached Kanji, the wave sucked up water from the island's shore, making the stones roar.

The liquid mountain of seawater towered higher, tottered, and then, with a sound like thunder, collapsed in a welter of foam. The collapsed wave came tearing up the hillside, carrying away the school as it came. The seawater chased the schoolchildren and their teacher up the slope.

Matthew John looked back and saw the wave coming after him. School desks and chalkboards bobbed in the froth. The floodwater rushed up the hillside towards him.

We are not going to make it, he thought. We are going to be swept away. He reached for his bat rider phone.

'The wave has arrived, Number One Squadron,' he said. 'If you are going to rescue us, now would be a good time.'

Something brown and furry crashed into the hillside in front of him.

'Bulmer!' said Matthew John.

'Oo!' said Bulmer. 'That hurt! I'm no good at landings. Jump onto my back, Matthew John.'

Matthew John leaped onto the back of his bat. 'Take us away, Bulmer!'

'Okay-dokey,' said Bulmer. He stretched his wings. 'Chocks away!' he said.

He was too late.

The wave hit them both.

'Obble bobble,' said Bulmer. 'Oogle boogle.'

Bubbles came out of his mouth. He flapped his wings in slow motion. I'm under the water, he thought.

Matthew John peered about him. His whole world had turned green. He was floating inside a cloud of shiny bubbles.

A bulletin board passed by, turning over very slowly in the current.

We're inside the floodwater, he thought. We must surface. We must breathe. I must not let go of Bulmer.

He heard a roaring in his ears. His brain raced. They were being sucked down deeper into the depths. He saw the hillside beneath him. He saw grasses waving like seaweeds. He fought his way back to the surface.

He opened his mouth and gulped in air. He bumped his head. He felt himself pulled back down under the water again. His head swam. His thoughts moved like lightning. He had to save both his bat Bulmer and himself. He hung onto Bulmer with one hand while he struck out with the other. He managed a few strokes.

If only the pounding in his head would stop and let him think. The seawater was cold. It was an effort to swim.

Matthew John and Bulmer popped up to the surface together. Matthew John swallowed another mouthful of air. He groped about with his free hand. His fingers closed around a leg of a floating school desk. He dragged himself up onto the top of the desk, and then helped Bulmer climb up beside him.

'Are you all right, Bulmer?'

Bulmer shook himself, sending drops of water

flying. 'I think so,' he said. He spat some water out of his mouth. 'What do we do now?'

Matthew John climbed onto Bulmer's back, put his arms around the bat's neck and gripped him tightly. 'We fly!' he said.

They sprang from the floating school desk into the air.

'How did you find me, Bulmer?' asked Matthew John. 'Miss Pretty Flower said that you were attending a navigation class.'

'Uh. I lost my way to navigation class,' said Bulmer, 'and then, when I saw the wave coming, I thought I'd better see if you were all right.'

'I'm glad you came for me,' said Matthew John.

'You saved my life. You are the best bat in the whole world. I hope the bat riders of Number One Squadron arrived in time to save the others.'

Akihito Akemi, riding his bat Suki, saw the great wave of seawater heading for Kanji Island.

'Ho, Suki!' he said. 'I see boys and girls running up the hill to escape wave. One girl is about to be drowned by the wave. We save that girl.'

'At once, honorable rider,' said Suki.

Akihito Akemi and Suki dropped from the sky and landed in front of Annabelle Sue.

'Who are you?' said Annabelle Sue.

'I am Akihito Akemi. This is my bat Suki. We are here to rescue you from great wave.'

'I want to be rescued by my *own* bat,' said Annabelle Sue, putting her hands on her hips. 'I want to be rescued by *Hula*.'

'No time to argue,' said Akihito Akemi, and pulled Annabelle Sue up behind him. 'Go, Suki!' he cried.

Akihito Akemi and Suki were just in time. As they took off, they felt the wave wet their feet.

Akihito Akemi looked about him. All the other ninety-nine riders were in the air, too. On the back of every bat sat two people. Every child in the school had been snatched to safety in the nick of time. The bat riders of Number One Squadron had done their duty. Their mission was a success, but Akihito Akemi could see no sign of the teacher, Miss Pretty Flower.

'Head back to the Hall,' he said into his bat rider phone. 'We must carry the children to safety.'

Obeying his order, the hundred bats of Number One Squadron wheeled through the sky and headed for home in a whir of beating wings.

As they left Kanji Island behind, Akihito Akemi thought he saw a large spotted creature swimming in the flood, carrying in its mouth something red.

He wanted to swoop down to investigate, but dared not break formation. He was the squadron leader, and it was his job to lead his fellow bat riders home.

Matthew John's parents were visiting the Hall of a Hundred Bats. They had been invited to a tea ceremony with Mr. Seeds. They had washed their hands and rinsed their mouths with water from a small stone basin. They had taken off their shoes, ducked their heads, and entered the Tea House through a small door. Inside the Tea House they had exchanged solemn bows with Mr. Seeds, and had watched him prepare thick tea on a charcoal fire. Now they were all drinking that thick tea from the same bowl, wiping the rim clean with a napkin before passing the bowl on to the next person.

Matthew John burst into the Tea House.

'Miss Pretty Flower is missing!' he cried. 'We could not save her from the wave. She was too heavy for our bats to carry.'

Mr. Seeds spun his chair around to face the boy. 'Tell us the story from the beginning, Matthew John,' he said. 'What is this wave of which you speak?'

Matthew John pulled himself together and explained about the warning from space, and the coming of the wave. He said what a good job Number One Squadron had done rescuing the schoolchildren.

'Thank goodness all of the young people are safe,' said Matthew John's mother.

Matthew John's father cleared his throat. 'You say that Akihito Akemi of Number One Squadron reported seeing a large spotted creature swimming in the floodwater and carrying something red in its mouth?' he said.

'Yes, Daddy,' said Matthew John.

'Akihito Akemi must have seen Miss Pretty Flower

being carried in the mouth of the leopard Hyou,' said Mr. Seeds, accepting the antique tea bowl from Matthew John's mother and putting it down gently on a brocaded cloth. He offered Matthew John a tray of tidbits from mountain and sea. 'Have you ever tasted sushi?'

Matthew John popped one of the tidbits in his mouth. It was wrapped in black seaweed and tasted of sea cucumbers and octopus. 'It's good,' he said. 'May I try another one?'

Mr. Seeds nodded.

Matthew John helped himself to another tidbit. This time it was a little cake stuffed with wild pigeon. 'Mmm,' he said, with his mouth full, chewing slowly to make the cake last as long as possible. 'Really good. Who is Hyou? Is he really a leopard? I don't think I've ever seen a leopard.'

'Hyou is the Leopard of Kanji. His fur is golden with black spots. His lair is on the island, at the very top of the hill. If you enter his lair, be careful not to touch his nose. Being touched on the nose is insulting to a leopard.'

'I'll try to remember not to touch his nose, Mr. Seeds,' said Matthew John.

'Matthew John,' said his mother, her eyes widening. 'Surely you are not planning to visit a leopard in his lair?'

'What else can I do, Mum?' said Matthew John. 'If Hyou has captured Miss Pretty Flower, then I have to do something. Miss Pretty Flower is my teacher. If it was you trapped in the leopard's lair, I would try to rescue you.'

Tears welled up in his mother's eyes. 'I know you would, Matthew John,' she said.

'Good luck, son,' said his father, shaking his hand.

'Thanks, Dad,' said Matthew John.

'One more thing,' said Mr. Seeds. 'Watch out for the snails.'

Matthew John and his fellow bat riders, reunited with their own bats, and very glad to be riding them, approached the island of Kanji from the north. They flew over the remains of their shattered school.

'Most of the water from the wave seems to have drained back into the sea,' said Joshua Ryan, flying his bat Smoky over crumpled rice paper walls and overturned desks.

'What a miserable mess!' said Vesper.

'We shall have to rebuild the school,' said Emily Charlotte.

'If we do, another wave will come and wash it away,' said Vesper.

'Not if we make the new school safe from floods,' said Annabelle Sue. 'Can we make it safe from floods, Hula?'

'Yes,' said her bat Hula. 'We can build a safe school.'

'Number One Squadron build new school,' said Akihito Akemi. 'My bat Suki is an architect. Suki make plan for new building.'

'The new school will have a brass gong, honorable master,' said Suki, 'and dragons.'

'First we rescue Miss Pretty Flower from that leopard,' said Matthew John. 'A new school is no good without a teacher, and we need Miss Pretty Flower back. You saw her being carried by Hyou to his lair?'

'A big furry animal with spots was swimming. He was carrying something red in his mouth,' said Akihito Akemi. 'That's all I know.'

'I expect Miss Pretty Flower has been eaten,' said Vesper. 'I expect the leopard was hungry.'

'I see the entrance to the leopard's lair,' said Matthew John. 'Follow me!'

The five bats landed in front of the entrance. Their riders leapt from their backs. They stared into a dark hole in the hill surrounded by crumbling rocks. The hole smelled of leopard.

Matthew John led the way down a narrow muddy underground passage. There was no room to fly. He could see paw prints in the mud. Each print had four toes. As he followed the paw marks, he spotted a big furrow. Something heavy had been dragged along through the mud. The passage widened into a round chamber. The walls of the chamber were crawling with grey slimy things with coiled shells that glowed green.

'Remember what Mr. Seeds said,' he whispered to his companions. 'Watch out for the snails.'

'What are snails?' asked Bulmer.

'A snail,' said Joshua Ryan, 'is an animal with a shell. It has no legs and one foot.'

'One foot?' said Bulmer. He plucked one of the

glowing snails from the wall and turned it over to have a look. 'How can you have a foot without a – '

The snail stabbed Bulmer with a love dart. 'Gotcha!' said the snail.

'Oo!' said Bulmer. 'I feel funny. I want to kiss everyone.'

'Bulmer, stop looking at me like that,' said Hula.

'You're beautiful, Hula,' said Bulmer, his eyes as big as saucers.

'Bulmer! Pull yourself together! We're in a leopard's lair,' said Matthew John. 'Try to keep your mind on our mission. We have to find our teacher, Miss Pretty Flower, remember?'

'Miss Pretty Flower!' said Bulmer. A dreamy look came into his eyes.

'Bulmer! Why are you plucking another snail from the wall?'

'Here, Matthew John,' said Bulmer. 'Have a snail. They make you feel wonderful.'

'No thanks,' said Matthew John. He turned his back on Bulmer and the snail. He ran down a passage that led deeper into the lair of Hyou. He had to find Miss Pretty Flower.

When his friends tried to follow him, hundreds of snails came rushing towards them, exuding slime and throwing love darts.

'Quick! Down here!' said Annabelle Sue. She grabbed Emily Charlotte by the hand and dragged her into a side tunnel.

They were in a storeroom.

Joshua Ryan dived behind a crate filled with turnips.

Thunk! Thunk! Thunk! Love darts hit the crate and quivered like spent arrows.

'I smell perfume,' said Emily Charlotte. 'I feel dizzy.'

'We're doomed,' said Vesper. 'We're falling in love.'

'The love darts are coated in romantic slime,' said Joshua Ryan. 'I read about it in a book.'

Smoky put his head above the crate for a quick look.

'The snails are coming. They are leaving shiny trails behind them.' He ducked down again.

'I hear them talking,' said Akihito Akemi.

'Lovey-dovey,' said one snail.

'Snuggly-wuggly,' said another.

'Kissy-kissy,' said a third snail.

'I hope Matthew John is all right,' said Hula. She raised her head to see where Matthew John had gone.

Thunk!

A love dart pinned her ear to the wall.

'Uh-oh!' she said. She smiled a foolish smile. 'I feel mushy,' she said.

Miss Pretty Flower woke. She sat up and looked about her. She was in a strange, dim grotto. Pillars glittering with crystals propped up an arched ceiling. Hundreds of grey snails with glowing shells were crawling up and down the walls. She scrambled to her feet and looked about her in amazement. How had she come to this odd underground place? Where were the schoolchildren? Were they safe? Why was she so wet? She wrung some water from her hair. She squeezed some more water from her kimono. She heard a scraping sound, and turned to face the sound, her heart in her mouth.

'Who's there?' she said.

'Hyou!' said a growly voice.

'Who?' asked Miss Pretty Flower. She peered into the dim recesses of the cavern. 'Show yourself, whoever you are.'

'If I show myself,' said the voice. 'Will you promise not to scream?'

Miss Pretty Flower folded her arms and looked stern. 'I am a teacher,' she said. 'Teachers do not scream.'

A monster stepped from the shadows.

The monster was a huge, wet leopard. Water ran down from its fur and pooled on the floor of the grotto. The leopard had golden fur with dark spots.

When the leopard opened its mouth to speak, Miss Pretty Flower saw a lot of teeth.

'Who are you?' she whispered.

'I am Hyou,' said Hyou. 'I am a mighty leopard but I am mightily ignorant. I do not know my times tables. I do not know who Little Miss Muffet was or why she sat on a tuffet, and I cannot sing "Oh, do you know the muffin man?" I hunger for learning. Will you help me, Miss Pretty Flower?'

Miss Pretty Flower was surprised that a leopard should want to go to school, but decided to help him if she could.

'I shall need my chalkboard if I am to teach you,' she said.

'Is this what you need?' asked Hyou, dragging

something big and flat from the shadows. 'I saved it from the school.'

'That's the very chalkboard I was writing on before the wave came. Let me see if I still have my stick of chalk in my pocket. Yes, I do.' She wiped the board clean with the sleeve of her kimono. 'Good,' she went on. 'Now we are all set. What would you like to learn about in your first lesson, Hyou?'

Hyou scratched his head. 'What is one plus one?'

'I'll show you,' said Miss Pretty Flower, and so the education of the leopard of Kanji began.

Matthew John felt his way down the dark tunnel deeper and deeper into the lair of Hyou. He was on his own. His friends had all been overcome by the love darts of the snails. The dark frightened him. He had been frightened of the dark for as long as he could remember. The thought of coming face to face with Hyou in the dark bothered him quite a lot. Suppose the leopard attacked him. Without his bat, how would he be able to escape? Not that he wanted to escape. What he wanted was to rescue his teacher, Miss Pretty Flower, but he had no idea how. He did not even know if Miss Pretty Flower was alive. He hoped very much that she was alive. He liked Miss Pretty Flower. She was a polite teacher who never shouted at anyone.

He heard voices.

He entered a large comfortable room, smelling of carrots and filled with the soft green light of the snails. It was a relief to be able to see again.

'How many quantum numbers define an orbital?' he heard Miss Pretty Flower ask.

'Three,' answered a growly voice.

'Good,' said Miss Pretty Flower. 'You are a fast learner, Hyou. I wish all my pupils were as quick as you. I'll write the equation for you.' She turned and wrote a bunch of numerals and letters on the board.

Matthew John was surprised to see his teacher and the leopard having a lesson. He cleared his throat.

'You're alive, Miss Pretty Flower,' he said. 'We were worried about you. It is good to see you safe and sound.'

'It is good to see you safe, too, Matthew John. I am alive thanks to Hyou here,' said Miss Pretty Flower. 'He is a good leopard. First he saved me from the flood and then he dragged me here to his lair, the only dry spot on the island.'

'How do you do, Hyou?' asked Matthew John, politely. He had never spoken to a leopard before.

'Very well thank you,' said Hyou. 'Your teacher Miss Pretty Flower has taught me reading, writing, and quantum mechanics.'

'Tell me, Matthew John,' said Miss Pretty Flower. 'Are the other schoolchildren safe?'

'They are, Miss Pretty Flower,' said Matthew John. 'Bulmer saved me, and the hundred bats of Number One Squadron saved the others. We are planning to rebuild your school.'

Miss Pretty Flower clapped her hands. 'How lovely!' she said. 'When the new school is ready, Hyou can join us there to continue his lessons.'

'I can?' said Hyou, scratching his head with his paw. 'Me? Go to school? The children won't scream when they see me? I am a leopard, you know.'

'I shall explain to them what you explained to me, that you are vegetarian leopard, and then I shall teach them what 'vegetarian' means.'

Hyou was happy. 'I'm going to go to school,' he said, and grinned at Matthew John.

'I expect you'll like it,' said Matthew John, and smiled shyly at the huge creature.

Hyou did a handstand. He could not believe his luck. He had always wanted to go to school. 'When the bell rings for recess, will I be allowed to go out in the playground?'

'Yes,' said Miss Pretty Flower.

Bulmer hobbled into the chamber, dreamy-eyed

and covered in romantic slime. 'I love you!' he said, and kissed the leopard on the nose.

Hyou knocked Bulmer over with a slash of his paw. He jumped on top of Bulmer. 'YOU STUPID BAT!' he bellowed. He brought his face very close to Bulmer's face. He opened his mouth wide to show his teeth. 'YOU KISSED MY NOSE!'

'You must be Hyou,' said Bulmer, and his eyes misted over. 'Marry me, Hyou!' he said.

'MARRY YOU?' said Hyou, leaping off Bulmer and backing away hastily. He pushed past Matthew John. 'I need some fresh air,' he said faintly.

'Come back, my ooky-wooky snookums!' said Bulmer. 'Come back, my love! I want to have baby snails with you.'

Bulmer got to his feet and hobbled after the leopard.

Matthew John found himself alone with his

teacher.

He scratched an itchy place on his knee and stared down at the muddy floor. He wanted to ask Miss Pretty Flower a question but he wasn't sure how.

'Uh, Miss Pretty Flower?' he began.

'Yes, Matthew John?' said the teacher and waited patiently. Sometimes her pupils found it difficult to ask her questions. She wondered what was on Matthew John's mind.

'Miss Pretty Flower, it's like this. In the beginning, I just wanted to be a bat rider. Then I volunteered to go into the Back of Beyond to rescue Chef Wandor's daughter, and brought her back safely, so the other bat riders voted for me to be their squadron leader.'

'They made a good choice,' said Miss Pretty Flower. 'I have noticed that you care about other people, and that you take your work seriously. Those are good qualities in a leader. Today you were brave. You came here to rescue me from the lair of Hyou, for which I am grateful. You thought Hyou dangerous, and risked your life for my sake.'

Matthew John looked up. 'But – ' he said. He paused. He bit his lip.

'Yes, Matthew John?' said Miss Pretty Flower, raising an eyebrow,

'After our mission to the Loony Moon, they made me a wing commander and I had to look after two squadrons,' Matthew John explained. 'Then the volcano erupted, and I led an expedition to the Lava Tubes of Boom, so they made me group captain, and I had to look after two MORE squadrons.'

84

'My goodness!' said Miss Pretty Flower. 'That is a lot of squadrons. I had no idea you had been given so much to do. You must be wondering if you can cope.'

'It didn't stop there,' said Matthew John. He tore his eyes from the floor and gazed earnestly at his teacher's face. 'When I went for my tour of duty in space, I was made the captain of the Artibeus as well. So now I have the crew of a starship to look after as well as four squadrons of bat riders.'

'I can see why you might be a little worried by so many responsibilities,' said Miss Pretty Flower, looking thoughtfully at the boy. 'You have had a lot heaped on your young shoulders. How do you feel about that?'

'I feel small and stupid,' said Matthew John, and he spread his arms wide, his palms up. 'I don't know how to look after so many people, and I am frightened some of them may get hurt because I don't know how to keep them safe.'

'Safe from what?' asked Miss Pretty Flower.

Matthew John closed his eyes. He put his fingertips to his forehead. 'When I was in space there was this message from a bunch of scary bats called the Mormoops.'

'Ah!' said Miss Pretty Flower. 'Now I understand. You fear an invasion. Would it help if I told your fortune?'

'My fortune?' said Matthew John, opening his eyes. He was puzzled.

'I can look into the future and give you an idea of what is coming,' Miss Pretty Flower explained. 'Would you like that?'

'Yes, please,' said Matthew John.

'Do you remember the names of the five elements of fortune telling that I wrote on the board this morning?' asked Miss Pretty Flower.

'Um, let me think,' said Matthew John, casting his mind back. 'There was Earth, Fire, Wind, Water and … Space.'

'Hyou saved my crystal ball from the flood,' said Miss Pretty Flower. 'Sit down, Master Mathew John, and breathe deeply.'

'Miss Pretty Flower told your fortune?' said Matthew John's mother, later that day.

'Yes,' said Matthew John.

In the Tea House of the Hall of a Hundred Bats, Mr. Seeds and Matthew John's Mummy and Daddy gazed at Matthew John in amazement.

'What did Miss Pretty Flower tell you?'

'I'm not allowed to say,' said Matthew John.

'How did you manage to get Bulmer and your other love-sick friends to return home?' asked Mummy.

'The effect of the snails' love darts wore off after a while, and they couldn't recall much of what had happened. When I told Bulmer he had kissed a leopard, he giggled.'

'Powerful creatures, the snails of Kanji,' said Mr. Seeds. 'I have prepared some thin tea. Would you care to try some? You will find the thin tea more refreshing than the thick.'

'Thanks,' said Matthew John. He took the bowl carefully and raised it to his lips. He sipped cautiously. The tea tasted of mint and seaweed. It warmed his tummy. He wiped the rim of the bowl with a napkin before he passed the bowl on to his mother.

'Have another tidbit,' said Mr. Seeds.

Matthew John helped himself to a round cake covered in toasted sesame seeds. 'Yum,' he said. 'Tuna.'

'I'm proud of you, Matthew John,' said his mother. 'You saved your whole school from drowning, and then braved a leopard's lair.'

'I was just lucky, Mum.'

'Lucky and brave,' said his father, clapping him on the shoulder.

'Thanks, Dad.'

'The Air Commodore has outgrown his bat, ' said Mr. Seeds. 'His job is yours now, Matthew John.'

'Oh, no,' said Matthew John. He groaned. 'You mean I've been promoted AGAIN?'

'Yes. Promotion happens pretty fast among bat riders. I do hope you are not feeling swamped?'

'I'll manage somehow, Mr. Seeds,' said Matthew John, avoiding the old man's eyes while busying himself pouring fresh tea from the teapot into the communal bowl.

'You are our best bat rider, Matthew John,' said Mr. Seeds. 'We are counting on you. I hear that a black ship is coming from a faraway world, a ship that may be dangerous.'

'I'll warn my bat riders and alert the Artibeus,' said Matthew John, wondering where to put down the teapot.

ARTIBEUS

89

CHAPTER IV

Saving the Yumi Trees

MATTHEW JOHN was having breakfast with his parents and Mr. Seeds. They were eating soft-boiled eggs and toast fingers.

'The vessel frightened the goats when it touched down,' said Mr. Seeds, looking out of his kitchen window at the huge black starship that had landed beside his house, squashing his blueberry bushes. 'The poor goats ran away into the forest.'

Matthew John dipped his toast finger in egg yolk and sucked it. 'What kind of starship is she?'

'I'm not sure,' said Mr. Seeds. 'When I was young, the oldest tree in the forest, First Seed, spoke to me of a black starship that would come to our world one day, bringing danger to us all,' said Mr. Seeds. 'This may be that ship.'

'I hope you not going to ask Matthew John to find out,' said Matthew John's mother. 'We don't know what kind of people are inside the ship.'

'I see a hatch opening,' said Matthew John's father, rubbing the steam of the kettle from the pane.

Matthew John swallowed his toast finger and joined his father at the window. He took his bat rider phone from his pocket. 'Annabelle Sue?'

'On my way, Matthew John,' said the voice of his friend. 'The pie is still hot.'

'I'll meet you by the black starship,' said Matthew John.

'Matthew John!' said his mother. 'What are you up to?'

'Don't worry, Mum. My friends and I are going to give our visitors a present, that's all.'

'You're not going to go inside that black starship?' said his mother, covering her face with her hands, and looking at him between her fingers.

'We'll be riding our bats,' said Matthew John. 'If there's any kind of trouble, we'll fly straight out again.'

'Mr. Seeds,' said Matthew John's mother. 'Please tell my son this is a job for grown-ups.'

Mr. Seeds wheeled his chair to the window and peered out at the black ship and its gaping hatch. 'I have come to have a great respect for your son,' he said, 'and to rely on him. As air commodore of the bat riders, the decision is his.'

Matthew John's father squeezed his son's shoulder. 'Think big and you won't be a pig.'

'Daddy!' said Matthew John. 'This is serious. We are going to negotiate with aliens.'

'If you are boarding the black ship,' said Mr. Seeds, searching in the cupboard where he kept his treasures, 'you had better take this with you, Matthew John.'

Mr. Seeds hung a small key on a chain around the boy's neck.

'What's this for?' asked Matthew John, looking down in wonder at the shiny gold key dangling on his chest.

Mr. Seeds gazed into the distance. 'When I was your age and a bat rider,' he said, 'First Seed told me to keep the key safe until the day the black ship returned. "Find the hourglass," she said. I had no idea what she was talking about, so I put the key in a safe place. Now, in case this should be the black ship of which she spoke, I am passing the key on to you. Use the key wisely, Matthew John.'

Matthew John's jaw dropped. 'You were once a bat rider, Mr. Seeds?' he said. 'You never told me.'

Mr. Seeds smiled. 'Better not keep your friend waiting.'

'Right,' said Matthew John. He grabbed another toast finger, stuffed it in his mouth and ran out of the house.

'I'm frightened for him,' said Matthew John's mother.

'So am I,' said Mr. Seeds. 'He is so young and has so many responsibilities.'

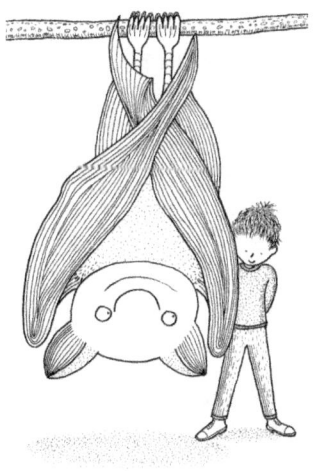

Matthew John's faithful bat Bulmer was waiting for him by the door. As a rule, bats are active at night and like to spend most of the day dozing, but Bulmer was not yet sleepy. 'Can we go inside the black ship now?' he asked.

'Yes,' said Matthew John, and jumped on

Bulmer's back. He hooked his hands together tightly under the bat's chin. 'Let's go!' he said.

Bulmer flapped his wings, did a Cobra Turn through the garden, narrowly missed a wheelbarrow, and rocketed fast and low across the bruised blueberry bushes to the open hatch of the black ship.

Matthew John's three best friends, Joshua Ryan, Emily Charlotte and Annabelle Sue, were waiting for him there, circling in the air. They had flown several missions with Matthew John, and were looking forward to starting this new one.

Annabelle Sue held a Yumi pie in one hand while she gripped the fur of her bat Hula with the other. 'This pie is a present from my father for the aliens inside the black ship,' she explained.

'Maybe the aliens don't like pies,' said Vesper, Emily Charlotte's sad-faced bat. 'Maybe they'll eat us instead.'

'Don't worry,' said Emily Charlotte, rubbing her bat's neck. 'I won't let them harm you.'

'What's that?' said Joshua Ryan, cupping his ear with his hand.

'Hush!' said Matthew John. 'Everybody listen.'

The four bat riders and their bats circled the entrance to the black ship, straining to hear.

'Alien music,' said Hula.

The four bat riders flew into the ship. An audience of huge, ugly bats hung by their feet from a steel grill on the ceiling, gazing at an empty stage. Beside each bat hung a stick with handles and a spring.

The music grew louder.

The bat riders landed quietly on the floor at the back of the hall. Nobody noticed. All eyes were on the stage.

The music stopped.

The bats hanging from the ceiling murmured among themselves, and then fell silent.

Hoomp-diddy! Hoomp-diddy!

'Someone's coming,' said Bulmer.

A bat bigger than any Matthew John had ever seen came bouncing onto the stage. He was balanced on a springy stick. As the springy stick hit the floor of the stage it went 'Hoomp!' and as it lifted the big bat up into the air it went 'Diddy!'

'My fellow bats,' said the big bat. 'Our long voyage is over, (bounce) and we have arrived (bounce) on this primitive planet (bounce) where the local bats have yet to invent the pogo stick (bounce).' The members of the audience rattled their pogo sticks and laughed.

'What's the big bat talking about?' asked Bulmer.

'Look at the thing he is bouncing on,' said Matthew John. 'It has foot rests, handles, and a spring.'

'Why doesn't he fly?' asked Bulmer.

'No idea,' said Matthew John.

'Three thousand years ago,' (bounce) the big bat went on, 'we planted Yumi tree seeds on this planet. (bounce) The trees we planted are now a mile high, (bounce) and are ready to be turned into pogo sticks.' (bounce)

'The local bats may not wants us to cut down their Yumi trees,' said a voice from the crowd.

'I don't care,' answered the big bat. 'That's why they call me BIG (bounce) BAD (bounce) BAT (bounce).'

The audience rattled their pogo sticks and chanted 'BIG BAD BAT! BIG BAD BAT! BIG BAD BAT!'

'Big bad idiot!' shouted Annabelle Sue.

She flew her bat Hula straight at the Big Bad Bat.

Big Bad Bat frowned at the sight of a strange little bat rushing through the air towards him beneath the heads of his dangling upside-down audience.

'Who are you, little bat?' he asked, frowning. 'Where's your pogo stick?'

'My name's Hula, and I don't have a pogo stick,' said Hula. 'I am flying.'

'Flying?' said Big Bad Bat, scratching his head. 'What does that mean? What is that creature clinging to your back?'

'She's a human child. Her name is Annabelle Sue, and she has a present for you.'

'A present for me?' said Big Bad Bat. 'I don't think that anyone (bounce) has ever (bounce) given me a present (bounce).'

'Surprise!' said Annabelle Sue, and threw the pie.

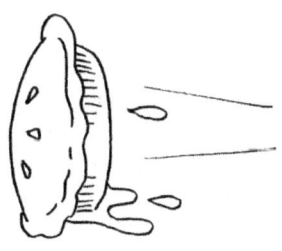

Nothing in Big Bad Bat's day had prepared him for being hit in the face by a pie. He had woken up early that morning and had lain awake playing with his pogo stick. While brushing his teeth, he had admired himself in the mirror. He had been delighted by the way the rubies on his pogo stick had caught the light as he had bounced. 'My, oh my!' he had said to himself, 'what a fine Big Bad Bat am I.'

He had tugged at a bell pull to summon his human slave. He was too fat to put on his coat by himself.

'Big day today, Addison Carter,' Big Bad Bat had said to his slave while he was being dressed. 'I told you we'd visit your home planet! (bounce) Fine crop of Yumi trees you've got here! (bounce) Can't wait to start cutting them down! (bounce) Ha, ha, ha!'

'The trees may not wish to be cut down,' Addison Carter had replied while pinning a ribbon across Big Bad Bat's chest. It is not easy to dress a bat that is jumping up and down on a pogo stick.

Big Bad Bat had laughed. 'I'll chop the trees down anyway, for I'm BIG and I'm BAD and I'm a BAT!'

'But Yumi trees are very important to my planet,' Addison Carter had dared to say. 'The trees provide my people with food, clothes and shelter.'

'Not after I've finished with them,' Big Bad Bat had replied, and he had bounced away to have his breakfast. After breakfast, Big Bad Bat had made a rousing speech, and his followers had rattled their pogo sticks happily. Everything had gone swimmingly until a funny little bat had appeared with a human child riding on its back.

Splat!

Something sticky hit Big Bad Bat in the face. He could not see. He lost his balance. He fell off his pogo stick and landed with a thump on the stage.

The audience gasped.

Big Bad Bat clawed sticky pie juice from his eyes, staggered to his feet, and shook himself. Bits of pie flew everywhere. He picked up his fallen pogo stick, hopped back onto it and began bouncing again. He saw the cheeky little bat whose rider had thrown the pie at him join three companions at the back of the hall.

Big Bad Bat called out to them: 'You three can't escape me, I'm BIG, I'm BAD and I'm COMING TO GET YOU!'

He bounced from the stage.

His followers grabbed their own pogo sticks and dropped from the ceiling. They went bouncing after their leader shouting 'We're BIG, we're BAD and we're COMING TO GET YOU!'

A chase began.

Hoomp-diddy! Hoomp-diddy! Hoomp-diddy!

Matthew John and his friends, riding their bats, flew down the companion-way of the black starship, the din of the pogo sticks of their pursuers ringing in their ears.

Matthew John wished he knew his way around the ship. His bat rider phone rang. He snatched the phone from his pocket. 'Yes?' he said.

'Take the third tunnel on your left, the one with blue crawly things.'

'Who's that?' said Matthew John, frowning.

'Misty.'

'Addison Carter's bat?'

'Yes.'

'May I speak to Addison Carter?'

'Later. Take the blue tunnel. Trust me. I know this starship like the veins on my wings.'

Matthew John steered Bulmer into the blue tunnel. 'Where next? The Big Bad Bat is still following us.'

'Watch for a gravity tube ringed by slugs.'

'I see it.'

'Go in and head down. I'll meet you in the hold.'

Matthew John flew Bulmer into the gravity tube. His friends followed, riding their own bats.

Big Bad Bat bounced after them.

The gravity tube was decorated with life-size moving pictures of Big Bad Bat riding on his jeweled pogo stick and waving to adoring crowds. Matthew John wanted to throw up. He and his friends tumbled slowly head over heels down the gravity tube.

'The alien bats don't fly,' said Joshua Ryan to Matthew John as they tumbled.

101

'They have wings,' said his bat Smoky, thoughtfully.

'True, but they seem to have forgotten how to use them,' said Emily Charlotte.

Matthew John and his friends hit the bottom of the tube.

Misty was waiting for them there. She pressed the REVERSE GRAVITY button and Big Bad Bat was sucked back up the tube.

'Quick!' said Misty. 'Before he comes back. What do we do?'

'Take us to your rider,' said Matthew John. 'Take us to Addison Carter.'

'This way!' said Misty.

She flew at breakneck speed among stacked crates of pogo sticks.

The bat riders slammed through a swing door made of green baize.

'This is where the slaves live,' said Misty.

Addison Carter was in his cabin putting a shine to Big Bad Bat's pogo helmet. He looked up when the bat riders burst in. 'Is this a rescue?' he asked.

'I remember you,' said Joshua Ryan. 'You are Addison Carter, the starship captain who gave up his ship to go to another world.'

'You are the captain who hates bats,' said Emily Charlotte.

'Of course I hate bats,' said Addison Carter. 'I polish Big Bad Bat's pogo helmet for him, but he doesn't wear it. Yes, Big Bad Bat. No, Big Bad Bat. Have a good day, Big Bad Bat. Don't forget your medals, Big Bad Bat. A curse on Big Bad Bat and on all his kind. Bats! I despise them. Good to see you again, Misty. Nothing personal.'

'I've missed you too, Addison Carter,' said Misty. 'Here's a friend of yours.'

'Matthew John,' said Addison Carter, putting down the Big Bad Bat's pogo helmet and rising to take Matthew John by the hand. 'You have indeed come to rescue me? How's my starship?'

'Yes, we have come to rescue you,' said Matthew John, 'and you'll be glad to hear that the repairs to the Artibeus have been completed. She's as good as new. But what of you? You were on your way to visit a world called Mormoops, as I recall.'

'Mormoops is run by a bat,' said Addison Carter.

Matthew John raised his eyebrows. 'Big Bad Bat?'

'Yes. The first thing Big Bad Bat said to me was: "How dare you ride on the back of a bat? Bats are not to be humiliated. We'll have no slavery here." So, like a fool, I climbed down from Misty's back, and from that moment on I was Big Bad Bat's slave.' Addison Carter shoved the Big Bad Bat's pogo helmet away from him in disgust.

'But why has Big Bad Bat come to visit our planet?' asked Matthew John, furrowing his brow.

'He has come,' said Addison Carter, looking Matthew John in the eye, 'to cut down all of the Yumi trees and turn them into pogo sticks. He'll do it, too. You should have seen the mess he made of the last place he visited.' Addison Carter lowered his voice. 'He has huge tree-eating machines.'

'What is Big Bad Bat afraid of?' asked Matthew John, rubbing his chin pensively.

'He does have nightmares,' said Addison Carter. 'I have to bring him a hot drink some nights.'

'Nightmares?' said Matthew John.

'He dreams of when he was a baby bat,' said Addison Carter, 'in bed with a fever, and saw his toy tiger looking in through his bedroom window.'

'We need a small tiger,' said Matthew John, and pressed the red BAT ALERT button on his phone. 'Akihito Akemi? Scramble your squadron. Your mission is to find Baagh the tigress. We need the help of her cub Kiti. Ask her to meet us outside Mr. Seeds's house.'

'I hear and obey, Air Commodore,' said the voice of Akihito Akemi. Over the phone came the sound of a bell being struck. Akihito Akemi was heard shouting 'Number One Squadron! To Hall of a Hundred Bats! Prepare steam catapults! Begin tiger hunt!'

Matthew shut his phone with a snap. 'So Big Bad Bat is after our trees.'

'His machines will destroy the trees,' said Vesper, 'and then we won't have any Yumi fruit, and we'll starve. I think I hear his pogo stick coming.'

'Jump on Misty's back, Addison Carter,' said Matthew John. 'We'll fly to a place where Big Bag Bat can't follow us. Where shall we go?'

'There is a forbidden chamber in the bows of the ship, a room with a golden door,' said Addison Carter. 'All the bats are frightened of that room. They call it the Room of Secrets.'

Big Bad Bat burst into cabin, riding on his pogo stick. 'I'm BIG, I'm BAD and I've GOT YOU!' he cried triumphantly.

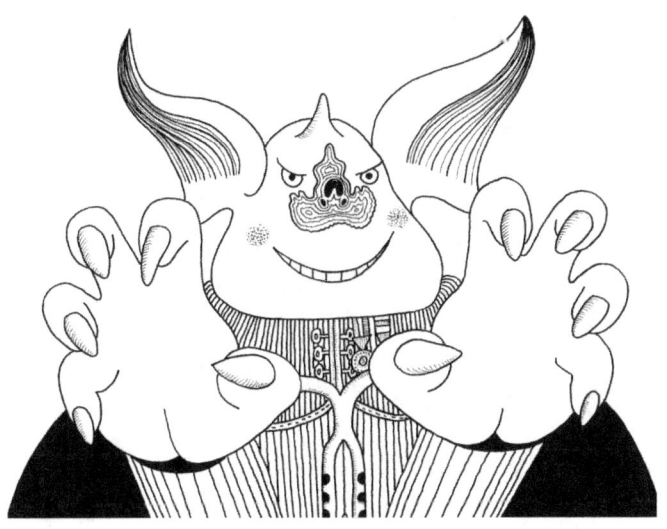

'Oh no you haven't, Big Bad Bat!' said Matthew

John, and the five bat riders darted past Big Bad Bat's head and shot out of the cabin.

Annabelle Sue tweaked Big Bad Bat's nose as she passed. 'You're SAD, you're MAD, and I'm going to tell my DAD!' she shouted, and added, over her shoulder: 'Next time I'll bung a banana split at you.'

'A BANANA SPLIT?' roared big Bad Bat.

The bat riders flew into the bows of the black starship. 'Look!' said Misty. 'There's the golden door!'

Matthew John leaped from Bulmer's back and fumbled for the golden key that Mr. Seeds had given him. He slid the golden key into the golden keyhole in the golden door.

'I'm turning the key,' he said.

'Stop!' shouted Big Bad Bat, who was bouncing towards them. 'You can't go in there. It's secret.'

Hiss!

The golden door rolled sideways and disappeared into the bulkhead as Matthew John pulled the key from the lock.

Joshua Ryan, Emily Charlotte, Annabelle Sue and Addison Carter and their bats fell into the Room of Secrets.

Bulmer threw himself after them.

Matthew John leaped into the Room of Secrets himself and hit the LOCK DOOR button.

Hiss!

The golden door rolled back out of the bulkhead and locked itself.

There was a thump and the rattle of a pogo stick as Big Bad Bat hit the other side of the door.

'We may not have much time,' said Matthew John.

They were inside a golden sphere. A golden hourglass floated at the room's heart.

'What can it be?' asked Emily Charlotte.

'I expect it's a death ray,' said Vesper.

Rays from the golden hourglass made bright spots on the golden walls.

'Has Big Bad Bat ever been in here?' Joshua Ryan wanted to know.

'He doesn't have a key for the door,' said Addison Carter.

The door shook. They heard the Big Bad Bat shout an order.

Matthew John made up his mind. 'I want that hourglass.' He jumped back onto Bulmer's back.

'Uh. Are you sure this is a good idea, Matthew John?' asked Bulmer.

They swooped to the heart of the chamber.

Matthew John reached out with his free hand and seized the golden hourglass. It felt warm and tingly.

'Bang on!' said Bulmer. 'We got the gold thingy.'

Bulmer looped the loop. Sparkly golden sand began to tumble from the upper part of the hourglass into the lower part.

The Room of Secrets darkened.

'Oh, dear,' said Vesper, faintly. 'I have a sinking

feeling about this.'

A tropical rain forest took shape around them. Ugly bats glided from one tree trunk to another. An unseen creature hooted. Another creature screeched like an owl.

An ancient bat stirred. She was hanging upside down by her feet from a branch.

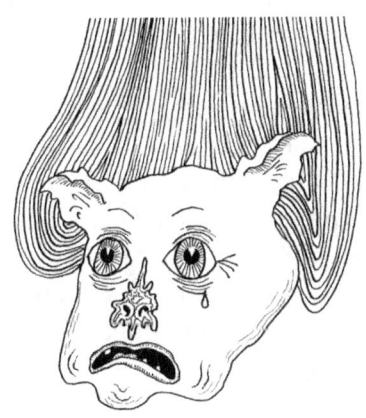

'My fellow bats,' she said in a quavery voice. 'This is the forest where we were born. Long ago, when our world of Mormoops was young, we crawled down from these trees and we built ourselves bat houses with bat chairs and bat beds. We thought we were clever. Bats had never lived in houses before. But to build our houses and our furniture, we cut down many of our trees.' She sighed. Her ears drooped.

The rain forest melted away, and through a triangular window Matthew John and his friends glimpsed a bat city festooned with suspended crawlways. There was not a tree to be seen.

'Then we built a starship so that we might sail out among the stars,' the old bat droned on, 'to teach those on other worlds to be as big and as bad as we were. But in our eagerness to improve ourselves, we cut down *all* of the trees on Mormoops. Without the life-giving gases exuded by the trees, the air of our planet grew thin and hard to breathe.' The old bat coughed.

The bat city vanished. Now there was nothing to be seen but dunes of sand stretching to the horizon under a dark sky sprinkled with stars.

'One wise bat named Wiggle saved a few seeds from the last of our trees, and set out in the starship to sow those seeds on other worlds, and to teach the inhabitants of those worlds to care for the trees that sprang up. You, my children, are Wiggle's descendants. This black ship is the vessel we sent out to seed distant worlds. Although we can no longer fly in the air of our own world, one day we hope to learn to fly again in the thicker air of some distant, unspoiled planet. Goodbye, my children, and good luck.'

The images vanished and the Room of Secrets brightened as the last grains of golden sand trickled down into the bottom half of the hourglass. Exactly one hour had passed.

Matthew John pulled out his phone and gave a string of orders.

A distant rumbling shook the ship.

'They are starting up the machines that will destroy the trees,' said Addison Carter.

'When I hit this UNLOCK DOOR button,' said Matthew John, jumping off Bulmer's back, 'I want you all to fly as fast as you can out of this golden Room of Secrets, down the companion-way and right out of this black ship into the fresh air. Everybody ready?'

'What about you, Matthew John?' asked Emily Charlotte. 'You're not mounted on your bat.'

'Don't worry about me,' said Matthew John. 'I'll be all right.'

'We're ready,' said Joshua Ryan and his bat Smoky, whizzing in a tight circle around the golden chamber.

'I'm ready, too,' said Emily Charlotte, taking off.

'So am I,' said her bat Vesper, 'in case anyone is interested.'

'Push the button!' said Annabelle Sue. She flew her bat Hula straight for the door.

Matthew John pushed the UNLOCK DOOR button, and the door slid open, revealing Big Bad Bat.

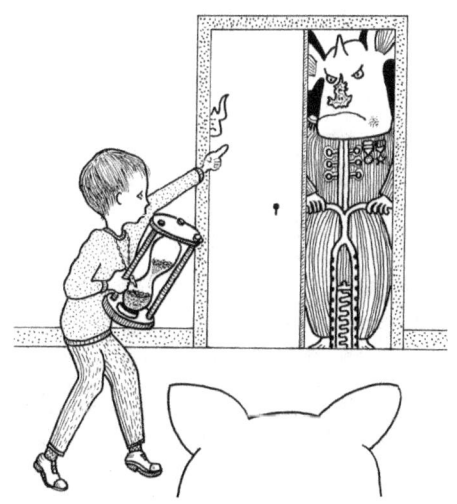

The golden door rolled aside.

Big Bad Bat bounced in. 'You are my prisoners,' he said. 'Hand over that hourglass.'

Annabelle Sue and Hula zipped between Big Bad Bat's ears. 'Big Bad Banana Split!' she said. 'Pity you can't fly!'

Big Bad Bat was furious. He gave a great leap on his pogo stick and hit his head on the ceiling.

'Aargh!' roared Big Bad Bat.

'You should have worn your helmet, Big Bad Bat,' said Addison Carter, as he and Misty flew by.

Big Bad Bat fell to the floor.

'Oof!' he said. He lost his grip on his pogo stick.

Bulmer picked up the pogo stick with his claws.

'Big Bad Nobody,' said Emily Charlotte, flying out of the door.

Big Bad Bat struggled to his feet. 'Come back! I'm BIG, I'm BAD …'

'And you're NUTS,' said Smoky as he and Joshua Ryan followed their friends out of the room.

Big Bad Bat turned on Matthew John and Bulmer, crouching by the door. 'Give me back my pogo stick!' he said, his eyes bulging.

'So this is your pogo stick?' said Bulmer, admiringly. 'Nice jewels. How do you make it work?'

'I put my feet on the bars, I hold onto the handles, and I straighten my legs,' said Big Bad Bat.

'Like this?' Bulmer leaped onto the Big Bad Bat's pogo stick, grabbed the stick by the handles, jammed his feet onto the bars and kicked down hard.

The pogo stick sprang over the top of Big Bad

Bat's head, carrying Matthew John, Bulmer and the hourglass out of Big Bad Bat's grasp.

'Hoomp-diddy!' said Bulmer. 'This is fun. I like pogo sticks!'

'Better give that stick to me, Bulmer,' said Matthew John.

The five bat riders shot out of the black starship and into the open air.

Something else shot out of the black ship, clattering and banging.

'What's that?' asked Matthew John, aghast.

'That is a tree-eating machine,' said Misty.

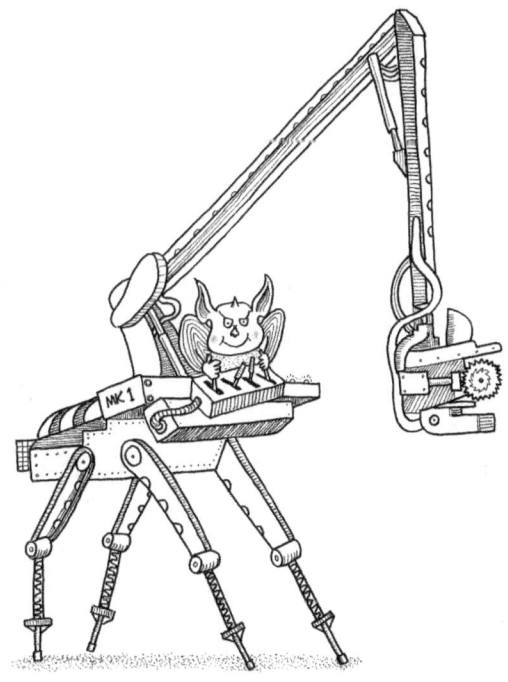

Hoomp-diddy! Hoomp-diddy! The machine was the size of an office tower. It stood for a moment wobbling on four spindly pogo stick legs, and then, when the bat hanging from the machine's driving seat pulled a lever, the machine began to bounce towards the nearest Yumi tree, unfolding a long metal limb tipped with circular saws.

'This is Air Commodore Matthew John calling all squadrons,' said Matthew John on his Bat Rider phone. 'The Yumi trees are under attack. All riders rendezvous with me by the black ship.' He pressed the button that put him in touch with his own starship. 'Communications! Put me through to the Emperor of the Moths.'

'Aye, aye, captain,' said the communications officer in the Artibeus. 'Putting you through.'

'Your Imperial Magnificence,' said Matthew John. 'Are you all set?'

'Yes, Matthew John,' said the Emperor.

'You may send your people down.'

A hundred thousand moths of the Imperial Guard fluttered down on powdery wings and settled on the driver of the machine, Small Bad Bat. The moths had prickly legs that tickled. Small Bad Bat wanted to brush the moths off but dared not let go of the levers with which he was operating his machine. Moths crawled into his ears. Moths crawled over his eyes.

'I can't hear!' he said. 'I can't thee! Thtop it! Go away, you thilly moths!' he said. 'Mmmph! Humph!'

One particularly daring moth crawled inside Small Bad Bat's mouth.

Small Bad Bat was fed up. He let go of the levers.

The machine tripped over a tree root, fell into the Back of Beyond, hit a rock and broke in two.

Small Bad Bat crawled out from the wreckage and spat the moth from his mouth.

'Thank you,' said the moth and shook her wings to dry them. She flew away to join her fellow moths.

Small Bad Bat leaped on his pogo stick. Hoomp-diddy! Hoomp-diddy! He vanished into a cave.

'Your moths were successful,' said Matthew John.

'I see a second machine coming,' said the Emperor.

Medium Bad Bat hung in the driver's seat of her brand new Mark Two Kill-a-Tree Harvester with Eezee-Think. Her machine had no levers. When she wanted her machine to do something, all she had to do was think about doing that thing, and the machine did whatever she wanted.

Start the power saws, thought Medium Sized Bad Bat.

The machine read her thoughts and started its power saws.

Jump forward, thought Medium Sized Bad Bat.

The machine read her thoughts and jumped forward.

Medium Bad Bat ran a comb through her fur and applied some gloss to her lips. Operating a machine was easy with Eezee-Think. If she wanted her machine to climb up to the top of the tallest tree that it could see, she was sure it would do just that.'

Her machine read her thoughts and climbed up the trunk of the tallest tree it could see. At the top of the tree, it found a tree garden.

'Have you come to kill me?' said a deep voice.

Medium Bad Bat saw a wrinkled face.

'Who are you?' she asked.

'My name is Boris. I am the tree whose trunk you just climbed. This is my treetop garden. I hope you like my swans. Would you care to taste one of my fruit?'

'They smell wonderful,' said Medium Bad Bat.

'Come down from your machine and I'll give you one.'

Medium Bad Bat unhooked her pogo stick, hopped onto it and jumped down onto a tree branch. Hoomp-diddy! Hoomp-diddy! She bounced along the branch.

The swans in the dewpond hissed at her and ruffled their feathers.

'Before I give you this fruit, will you promise to save the seeds?' asked Boris.

'I promise,' said Medium Bad Bat.

'This one is ripe and juicy,' said Boris, and offered Medium Bad Bat a sun-warmed fruit with his twiggy hand.

'Your fruit are shaped like stars,' said Medium Bad Bat, turning the fruit over in her claws. She bit into it. 'Ith yummy,' she said with her mouth full.

'I am curious,' said Boris. 'How do you control that machine of yours? I can't see any levers.'

Medium Bad Bat swallowed a mouthful of fruit. 'I think about what I want the machine to do and the machine does it.' She wiped some juice from her chin.

'Suppose you thought of your machine walking off the end of my branch?'

Medium Bad Bat laughed. It was funny talking to a tree. The thought of her tree-eating machine walking off the end of the branch made her giggle. Boris was a tree about a mile high and her tree-eating machine would not survive so long a fall. 'I'd better not think about my machine doing anything like that,' she said.

'You just did,' said Boris.

The Mark Four Kill-a-Tree Harvester stepped off the end of the branch. It tumbled down through the air, flailing its limbs and revving up its power saws, hit the ground and shattered into a hundred pieces.

The watching bat riders applauded.

Medium Bad Bat hopped to the end of the branch and looked down. 'Oh dear, my boss is going to be displeased with me for wrecking my machine. Here he comes now, Big Bad Bat himself,' she said, 'driving a Mark Three.'

Big Bad Bat's machine leaped from the black starship and stood swaying on Hoomp-diddy legs the size of battleships. Big Bad Bat was in the driver's seat. He was upset. His day was not going well. He had just seen two of his best tree harvesting machines brought down. He snarled. He would teach this planet a serious lesson. He would fell *all* of her trees.

After he had felled all of her trees, he would drag her miserable bats from their caves and teach them to be civilized and to live in proper houses. And as for the wretched humans who had dared to ride on the backs of the bats, he would show them the true meaning of slavery. He clenched his claws.

'I'm BIG,' he growled.

Gouts of flame shot from his machine and bushes burst into flames.

'I'm BAD,' he said.

Mechanical grapples seized one of Boris's tree roots and wrenched the root from the ground. Power saws screamed and sawed the root in two.

'And I'm a BAT,' he roared, and sent a steel ram shooting forwards on pistons. The ram thumped into Boris's trunk. Boris shook. Dozens of Yumi fruit came crashing down. They exploded as they hit the ground.

Big Bad Bat licked his lips. He could taste fruit juice.

'Ha-hah!' said Big Bad Bat. 'That'll teach you.'

Boris gave a groan. There was a mighty stirring of limbs and a sighing of leaves throughout the forest, as if the blow that Big Bad Bat had delivered to one of their kind had shocked all of the other trees.

Big Bad Bat frowned. Did these trees talk to one another? What kind of a planet was this? He looked up and saw hundreds of bats in fighter formation moving through the air making odd up-and-down motions with their wings. It was an uncanny sight. Bats without pogo sticks! Why did they not fall from the sky? And the weirdest thing of all was that every bat had a human rider.

'Leave that tree alone!' shouted one of the riders.

'You can't tell me what to do!' Big Bad Bat shouted back. 'I'm BIG BAD BAT!'

'I *am* telling you what to do,' said Matthew John, for it was he who was circling overhead. 'I'm Matthew John. Go back to your ship!'

'Why should I? I have a forest to fell, you silly little human.'

'You were silly and little yourself once,' said Matthew John. 'Have you forgotten? You were Little Baby Bat then, and you went to bed with a fever. Do you remember?'

Big Bad Bat broke out in a sweat. 'I don't know what you're talking about,' he said. He was lying.

'Be afraid, Big Bad Bat,' said Matthew John, and he made an upward motion with his free hand. 'Be very afraid.'

'What are you doing?' asked Big Bad Bat, biting at his claws. 'Who are you making that signal to? What is going on?'

'You don't want to know, Big Bad Bat,' said Matthew John, and he squeezed Bulmer's sides with his knees.

'But you're going to find out,' said Bulmer, taking the hint. Bulmer had to beat his wings fast to hover in the air out of reach of the long limbs of Big Bad Bat's machine.

A cardboard box drifted out of the forest.

'Purp,' said the cardboard box.

The box floated through the air towards Big Bad Bat.

'What's that?' whispered Big Bad Bat, staring at the box drifting towards him. He wiped sweat from his forehead with one of his wings. 'This can't be happening! I must be dreaming.'

The cardboard box floated nearer.

'Want to see what's inside the box?' asked Matthew John.

'No,' said Big Bad Bat. 'Make the box go away. That's an order.'

'I don't take orders from you, Big Bad Bat,' said Matthew John.

A growly voice spoke from the box: 'I am your toy

tiger.'

Big Bad Bat bit his lip.

'Bounce for your life,' said the tiger.

'I can't bounce,' said Big Bad Bat. 'I'm too frightened.'

'Use your legs,' growled the tiger.

'My legs?'

'Bats can crawl. Crawl back to your ship.'

'Me? The greatest bat who ever lived? Crawl?'

'Look at me, Big Bad Bat,' growled the voice from the box.

'Do I have to?'

'Yes.'

Big Bad Bat took a quick peep.

The head of a tiny tiger had appeared over the rim of the box. 'I'm SMALL, and I'm SCARY and I'm LOOKING IN YOUR WINDOW,' said the tiny tiger.

Big Bad Bat covered himself with his wings and burst into tears. 'I want my Mummy!' he wailed.

Two hundred bats on pogo sticks bounced out of the black starship to rescue their weeping leader. They dragged Big Bad Bat from his seat on the Mark Five machine and carried him on board.

As the door of the black ship began to close, Matthew John heard Big Bad Bat shout 'I won't give up, Matthew John! You wait! I'm BIG, and I'm BAD, and I'll be BACK!'

The black starship lifted off and headed out into space.

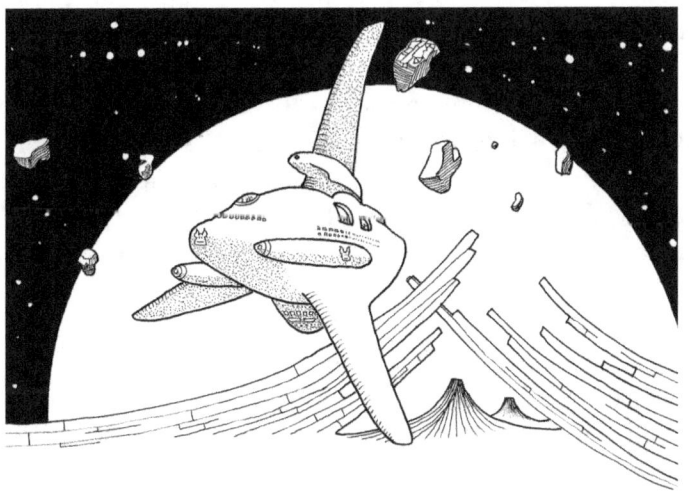

'Are you all right?' asked Matthew John's mother.

'I'm fine,' her son replied, 'thanks to Bulmer, who stole Big Bad Bat's pogo stick.'

'You are all heroes,' said Matthew John's father. 'Well done, Matthew John. I'm sorry about Boris. It must have been sore for him having his root sawn off.'

'Keep still, Boris,' said Mr. Seeds. 'This won't hurt.'

'I am a tree,' said Boris. 'We trees are good at keeping still.'

Matthew John held the lamp closer. He had never watched an operation before. Part of him wanted to look at what Mr. Seeds was doing, and part of him did not want to see.

With a sharp knife Mr. Seeds made a V-shaped cleft in the part of the root still attached to Boris. 'There!' he said. He wiped tree sap from his knife with a rag. 'Now we attach the severed root.'

'How?' asked Matthew John, swallowing.

'First we shape the sawn-off end of the root into a wedge to fit into the V-shaped cleft,' said Mr. Seeds, whittling away. 'There. That should do. Now we slide the wedge carefully inside the cleft. Can you help me, please, Matthew John? I need you to hold the two parts of the root tightly together.'

'Like this?'

'That will do, thank you. Keep on holding tight, please,' Mr. Seeds rolled his chair into his workshop, rummaged about in a drawer for a length of woven Yumi bark, and then returned carrying the bandage in his lap. 'Now we bind the two parts of the root together.' He put a dab of Make-You-Better butter on the tender place, and then wound the bandage round and round. 'How does that feel now, Boris?' he asked, making fast the end of the bandage with sticking plaster.

'It feels much better, thank you,' said Boris.

'Withdraw your root.'

The bandaged root slipped out of the window like a departing snake.

'Big Bad Bat said something as he left,' said Matthew John. 'He said he'd be back.'

'I wouldn't be surprised,' said Mr. Seeds. 'We have his hourglass.'

'I think you did very well,' said Matthew John's mother, holding her son by his shoulders and looking into his eyes.

'Very well indeed,' said his father. 'I expect they'll promote you again.'

'Thanks, Mum,' said Matthew John. 'Thanks Dad. It was all Bulmer's doing, really. You should have seen him when he leapt onto Big Bad Bat's pogo stick. It was really something.' He laughed. 'We sprang right over Big Bad Bat's head.'

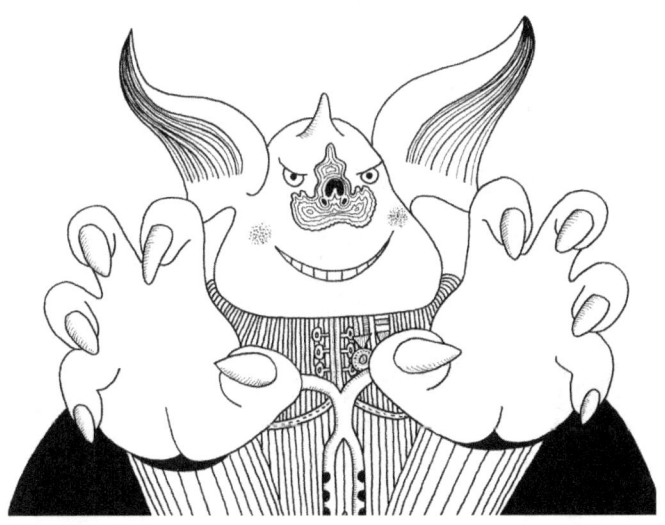

CHAPTER V

The Enchanted Grove

I N A TANGLE of arms, legs and wings, Matthew John and Bulmer splash-landed in the pool.

'Are you all right, Bulmer?'

'Bit of a ropey landing,' said the bat. 'Sorry.'

'What happened?' said Matthew John.

'You were too heavy for me to carry,' said Bulmer.

Matthew John looked about him. The cave where he lived had grown smaller. He ran up the Crystal Stair to the office he used to direct the activities of six squadrons of bat riders. The room had become less roomy, and the ceiling lower. He bumped his head on the lintel. He furrowed his brow. The arms of his chair had drawn closer together, and the pencil on his desk felt thinner. He had to scrunch up his eyes to read his own writing on the operations board. 'Number Five Squadron harvests Yumi fruit in the Old Forest tonight,' the board said.

Bulmer flew into the room and hung himself up to dry. Water dripped from his folded wings and made a puddle on the floor.

A girl wearing a yellow dress ran into the office. 'I want to be a bat rider,' she said, and did a handstand.

'Welcome to our cave,' said Matthew John. 'I'm Matthew John. Who are you?'

'Hannah Brianna,' she said, turning the right way up. 'Where's my bat? I need a bat. I'll have that one up there, the one hanging from your ceiling.'

'That's *my* bat.'

'I'll share him with you,' said Hannah Brianna. 'How do I get on his back?' she said.

'I'll help you,' said Matthew John. He lifted Hannah Brianna up. She was small and light. He turned her upside down and placed her on Bulmer's back. 'Put your arms around the bat's neck.'

'Your bat's wet,' said Hannah Brianna, frowning.

'Hang on tight, Hannah Brianna!' said Bulmer, and flew out of the office.

Hannah Brianna hung on for dear life. 'Wooee!' she said.

The bat and the girl sailed through the Hall of Lemon Yellow Moss.

Matthew John was reminded of his own wild flight on Bulmer's back when he had first come to the Cave of Oomba. Since then he and Bulmer had flown to the Back of Beyond, explored the Loony Moon, dived into Big Cat Canyon and sped through the lava tubes of Boom. They had been to the Pit of Mormoops, dared the lair of the leopard of Kanji, and driven off the Big Bad Bat. It was going to be strange not to have Bulmer to ride. He was going to miss him. He wondered where Bulmer had taken Hannah Brianna.

Bulmer had flown Hannah Brianna to her home and had found her parents there on the lawn, talking to Matthew John's parents.

'He's going to be my bat for ever and ever,' Hannah Brianna told them. 'His name is Bulmer.'

'But what of Matthew John?' asked Matthew John's father. 'Bulmer used to be his bat. How will he manage without a bat to ride?'

Matthew John was wondering the same thing as he made his way down to the mess hall. Chef Wandor was visiting from the Artibeus, and wonderful smells filled the air. Matthew John rubbed his hands together as he seated himself on the bench beside his friend Annabelle Sue. 'What are we having?' he asked.

'Jellied Moose Nose and Cupcake Frostyboots,' said Annabelle Sue.

A bat from the kitchen named Pipi flew low over their heads and placed a platter of Jellied Moose Nose on the table before them.

'Thanks, Pipi,' said Matthew John, helping himself to a slice. 'Mmm! Not bad.'

After he had finished his Cupcake Frostyboots dessert, he climbed up his rope to the briefing room.

The Loony Moon was full and filled the briefing room with light.

Bulmer made a clumsy landing on the stage and let Hannah Brianna slide from his back.

'You won't forget me, Bulmer?' asked Matthew John.

'I won't forget you,' said Bulmer. 'Will you forget me?'

'Never in a million years. Perhaps we could meet sometimes?'

'Okay-dokey,' said Bulmer.

'Bulmer, before I give you a goodbye hug, I want to present you with this medal that my Group Captain gave me.' Matthew John fished the medal from his pocket. 'Tuck in your wings, dear Bulmer, and try to look serious. This is a medal for being the best bat in the whole world.' He hung the medal around Bulmer's neck. 'There,' he said.

Bulmer looked down at his medal. He looked at the audience. His eyes grew big and round.

Bat riders seated in the curved tiers of the briefing room stamped their feet.

'Better not keep your new rider waiting, Bulmer,' said Matthew John, sensing that this was a turning point in his life. Recently his teacher Miss Pretty Flower had told him his fortune: 'One night you shall see your dream fly away.' Was this the night she had prophesied? It felt like it was. It felt weird. He had lost

131

both his bat *and* his command. Suddenly he was nobody. He had nowhere to go and nothing to do. He no longer mattered. Other, younger boys and girls would look after his bat rider squadrons now. He straightened his shoulders and cleared his throat. 'Bat Riders of Oomba,' he said, addressing those seated before him. 'I am proud of you and prouder still to have served as your squadron leader and your commodore.'

When the clapping ended, members of the audience carried Matthew John to the Old Forest in his hammock.

This had become a tradition among the boys and girls who harvested the Yumi fruit. Bat riders who had grown too big to fly their bats were taken to the Old Forest and abandoned there in the Enchanted Grove on the night of the full moon. Nobody knew why this was done, nor what became of those who did not return to their homes and to their parents.

    They left Matthew John at the base of a great tree in the Enchanted Grove. By the light of the Loony Moon Matthew John glimpsed the pillars of the world. The pillars were so broad that he could barely detect their curvature. Matthew John wondered how many hours it would take to walk around one of them. Somewhere among these giants must stand the oldest of all the Yumi trees, First Seed herself. He had heard about First Seed at school and had hoped to meet and question her some day, but now that seemed unlikely. What a shame! He might have learned much from First Seed. He had heard that she had memories going back thousands of years.

It was lonely in the Enchanted Grove. For a while he found comfort in the company of a wood mouse. After the mouse went on about its business, he listened to the cries of the bats and their riders foraging for Yumi fruit in the tree gardens a mile overhead, but then there came a great fluttering of wings as the foragers headed back to the Cave, and Matthew John clenched his fists. His nails bit into his palms. He hoped whoever was in charge had remembered to count the bat riders and to make sure no rider or bat was left behind. He was cold. He shivered. He did not like being in the dark, even when the moon was full.

A falling Yumi fruit struck branch after branch as it tumbled down to land at last with a soft thump on the mossy forest floor. After that, the grove fell silent. He stood in a patch of moonlight and he waited. He felt foolish, all by himself. What was he waiting for? What was he supposed to do? What became of riders who grew too big for their bats and were left here all alone in this strange grove?

He missed his work.

As Air Commodore, he had complained about having too many responsibilities, and having to remember the names and faces of all the bats and riders in his squadrons and in his school. He had even complained about having to take care of so many people at once. Now none of that mattered anymore.

He missed his parents.

His parents had no idea he was out here all by himself, unless Bulmer or Hannah Brianna had told them. He had been too ashamed to call his Mum and Dad himself. He had not wanted them to know he was no longer Air Commodore.

He missed his friends.

He wished Joshua Ryan were here to tell him how to find his way home. Joshua Ryan was clever with numbers, and would know how to use his bat rider watch to point the hour hand at the moon and figure out which way was north.

He would love to hear Emily Charlotte laugh. Emily Charlotte would think that a bat rider who was too big to ride his own bat was a hoot, and would tell some silly joke about it.

He would like talk to Annabelle Sue again. She would look him in the eye and say 'Well, Matthew John? I assume you have thought of a way out of this forest?' to which he would answer lamely 'I'm thinking something up' knowing full well that Annabelle Sue would not wait for him to make a plan, but would go ahead and act on her own.

He smiled. Even though his friends were absent, it cheered him to think of them.

Above all, he missed his bat Bulmer.

It had been Matthew John's fault that he had become too heavy for Bulmer to carry. He had eaten too many Yumi pies and had put on weight. Hannah Brianna would be a lighter load. He hoped that she and Bulmer would have many wonderful adventures.

He heard a wolf howl.
Wow-ooo-raa-ah!
He heard other wolves join in the howling.
Wow-ooo-raa-ah! Wow-ooo-raa-ah!
Matthew John bit his fingernails.
Wolves!

Loopy, the leader of the wolves, stopped to sniff the ground, his fur gleaming silver in the moonlight. His wife Loo ran to his side.

'Loo,' he said. 'Do you smell what I smell?'

His wife licked her lips. 'Cupcake Frostyboots. Must be a bat rider.'

Loopy leaped over a fallen tree. 'I'll eat the bat rider, and you can have his bat.'

Loo grinned. 'Wow-ooo-raa-ah!' she howled. She was fond of bats. They were crunchy.

Loopy and Loo began to run.

Their six sons and daughters speeded up to keep pace with them.

Wolves hunt in family packs. They begin to hunt at dusk and go on until their hunger is satisfied. They feast on meadow voles and snowshoe hares, but sometimes tackle larger prey.

Loo's eldest son, Bonkers, wanted to go in front.

'You're treading on my tail, Bonkers,' said Loopy.

'Out of my way,' said Bonkers. 'I want to be Lord of the Wolves.'

'Don't speak to your father that way, Bonkers,' said his mother. 'He's the Alpha Male.'

'I'll be the Alpha Male one day,' said Bonkers.

'Not if you tread on your father's tail, you won't,' said his mother. 'Now let's hear you howl.'

'Wow-oo!' said Bonkers.

'That wouldn't frighten a spider,' said his mother. 'You have to mean it. Listen to me: Wow-ooo-raa-ah! Wow-ooo-raa-ah!'

'Wow-oo-ra!' said Bonkers. 'I thought we were pretending to be sheep.'

The wolves leapt over a stream.

In the Enchanted Grove, Matthew John stepped out of the moonlight and crouched in the shadows, where he would be more difficult to see. His ears strained.

'It was somewhere around here that they set him down,' said a voice.

'What did the wolf say to the bat rider?' said a second voice.

'It's been nice gnawing you,' said a third.

'There he is,' said the first voice. 'He's still alive. Hi, Matthew John!'

'Annabelle Sue?' said Matthew John. 'I don't believe it. And Emily Charlotte and Joshua Ryan! What are you three doing here in the middle of the night in the Enchanted Grove? Where are your bats?'

'Joshua Ryan talked us into it,' said Annabelle Sue.

'We didn't want to leave you alone,' said Emily Charlotte.

Joshua Ryan regarded Matthew John seriously and said 'Scientifically speaking, if your bat Bulmer can't carry you because you have grown too heavy for him, then the same must be true for my bat Smoky, Emily Charlotte's bat Vesper, and Annabelle Sue's bat Hula, for we are all about the same age and we are all growing heavier by the day.'

'True,' said Matthew John. 'We can't help growing up.'

'That is why we asked our bats to fly us here and leave us,' Joshua Ryan went on. 'Our bats must be back at the Cave by now.'

'It wasn't easy saying goodbye to them,' said Annabelle Sue, 'so this had better be good, Matthew John.'

'You have arrived just in time,' said Matthew John.

Wow-ooo-raa-ah! Wow-ooo-raa-ah!

'What's that?' asked Emily Charlotte.

'Wolves,' said Matthew John. 'Coming to eat us.'

'We've arrived in time to be eaten by wolves?'

'Yes.'

'There must be somewhere to hide,' said Emily Charlotte, looking about hopefully.

'Hiding won't help. Wolves hunt by smell,' Joshua

Ryan reminded her.

'Your plan, Matthew John?' said Annabelle Sue.

'There's nowhere we can hide where the wolves won't find us,' said Matthew John, 'unless…'

'Unless what?'

Matthew John took his bat rider phone from his pocket. 'Artibeus? Ah, Crystal. How are you doing? All those hours in the navigation wind tunnel have given you a stiff back? That's too bad. I'm really sorry for you. Listen, Crystal. I need you to do me a good turn. I want you to put me through to First Seed, the oldest tree on the planet. Will you do that? Thank you. First Seed? Can you hear me?'

'You must be Matthew John,' said a voice. 'I've heard stories about you.'

The bat riders looked at one another. Was this the voice of the oldest tree in the world? It was a strong, confident voice, a voice that made one think of growing things and of springtime.

'Is that really you, First Seed? How kind of you to answer my call. I'm here in the Enchanted Grove with three of my friends, and a pack of wolves is closing in on us. Can you help?'

'Would you like to experience some of my oldest memories?' asked First Seed. Matthew John put his hand over the phone. 'She wants us to show us her memories.'

'What does that mean?'

'No idea.'

'Tell her yes,' said Annabelle Sue. 'Tell her to hurry up. Whatever she has in mind, it has to be better than being eaten by wolves.'

'First Seed?' said Matthew John into the phone. 'Yes, we like to do whatever you have in mind. Thank you.'

'Find the knot,' said First Seed.

Matthew John closed the phone and returned it to his pocket. 'She wants us to look for a knot.'

'A knot?' said Emily Charlotte. 'Are you sure she said a knot?'

Wow-ooo-raa-ah! Wow-ooo-raa-ah!

The wolves dashed into the grove, their eyes shining greenish-orange.

Keeping their faces towards the wolves, the four bat riders backed up to the nearest and largest of the trees.

Behind her back, Annabelle Sue explored the tree's bark with her fingertips. She found a knot in the wood and pressed it with her thumb. A gap appeared between two buttress roots. 'There's a door,' she whispered.

The wolves dashed towards them, slavering.

'Open the door,' said Matthew John. 'Quickly!'

The four bat riders pushed their way inside the tree, and shut the door behind them.

The wolves, cheated of their prey, whimpered and scrabbled at the outside of the door.

'The wolves know we are in here. They will scratch and claw until they force their way in,' said Joshua Ryan.

'Then we must find another way out,' said Matthew John, craning his neck and staring upward curiously. He had never been inside a tree before.

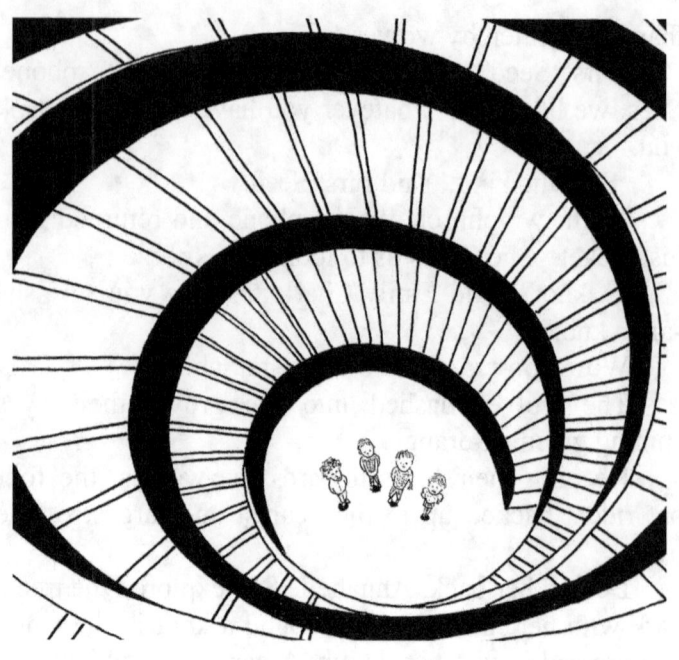

The tree was hollow and echoed with strange cries. A wide, rising ramp spiraled around the inside wall of the tree, wending its way upward. Far away and blue with distance, the same ramp could be seen climbing steeply like the threads of a huge screw. Matthew John was amazed.

The scrabbling intensified. The wolves were breaking through.

'This way!' said Matthew John, and ran up the ramp. His friends ran after him.

'Life begins,' said the voice of First Seed. Her voice came from high above their heads and boomed inside the tree.

The floor of the ramp contained steaming pools

bubbling with froth. In the pools, living things jiggled. Matthew John and his friends dashed through a curtain of sea lettuce, and dangling tendrils of jelly stung their faces and hands.

Annabelle Sue held her nose. 'Whatever thith thtuff in the poolth ith, it thtinks,' she said.

'Primordial soup,' said Joshua Ryan, slowing down to dip one of his fingers in the goop. 'Mmm. It tastes salty.'

'Keep running,' said Matthew John. 'We must stay ahead of those wolves.'

So they ran on up the slope. Sweat ran down their foreheads and into their eyes.

'Fishes leave the water and learn to run,' boomed First Seed.

Matthew John and his friends were swept off their feet by a charging shoal of fishes with legs. The ground began to shake. Something huge was coming down the ramp towards them! The fishes ran for cover beneath tree ferns.

'We have been sent back to a time out of mind,' said Emily Charlotte, admiring the primeval forest.

'A time out of First Seed's mind perhaps,' said Matthew John.

'The Age of Reptiles dawns!' said First Seed.

A dinosaur came dashing down the ramp towards them.

'It has three horns on its head,' said Joshua Ryan.

'What do you call a dinosaur with three horns on its head?' asked Emily Charlotte.

'Ouch-y-opteryx,' said Matthew John.

'Make-you-saurus,' said Annabelle Sue.

'Triceratops,' said Joshua Ryan, who knew the proper Latin name for the creature.

'Follow me!' said Matthew John. 'We'll climb up on its back!'

'Watch out!' shouted Emily Charlotte.

They leaped for safety as the beast's tail swung.

'That was close!' said Annabelle Sue.

They left the triceratops behind.

'The further up the ramp we go, the further we advance in time,' said Joshua Ryan, thinking out loud. 'First came the ooze, then the fishes with legs, then the dinosaurs...'

'And after the dinosaurs?' said Matthew John, his chest heaving. He was out of breath. It is not easy to run up a ramp.

'The world freezes,' announced First Seed.

Snow! Matthew John tilted his face upward, opened his mouth and felt a snowflake tickle his tongue. His feet slipped. He slid.

Emily Charlotte turned blue. She crossed her arms

over her chest and gripped her shoulders. 'Brr!' she said.

'Put your hands under your armpits,' said Matthew John. 'That way your fingers will warm up.'

'Thanks, Matthew John,' she said. 'That does feels better, but what about you? Aren't you chilly?'

'I'll manage,' said Matthew John, trying to stop his teeth chattering. With luck the Ice Age would not last long. His fingers were turning yellow, and he could not feel his toes.

The bat riders made their way up the frigid slope of the ramp, their footfalls muffled by the snow.

'I hear thumping feet,' said Annabelle Sue.

Five hairy creatures sixteen feet high stampeded out of a glacial grotto. One of the hairy creatures lifted a long trunk and trumpeted.

Waaaayow! Waaaayow!

'Woolly mammoths!' said Joshua Ryan.

The shaggy creatures vanished down the ramp into the snowstorm.

Something had startled those mammoths.

'Listen!' said Matthew John. He held up his hand and his friends came to a halt.

Hoomp-diddy! Hoomp-diddy! Hoomp-diddy!

'Uh-oh,' said Emily Charlotte. 'I've heard that sound before.'

'The sound is coming from in here,' said Matthew John, and ran inside a white-domed cavern with an ice-green river rushing through it. There were numerous waterfalls in the cavern, a natural arch of stone, several tunnels and a cascade that plunged down into the depths, carrying the water away. There was a big pool fed by a hot spring. The bat riders made their way carefully along the edge of the cascade. As they came to the pool, they heard fierce whispering.

'Hello?' said Matthew John, loudly. 'Who's that talking?'

'We're not here,' said a voice.

'We're bad bats!' said another voice. 'Go away!'

'We don't need you humans,' said a third voice. 'You just want to make us into slaves.'

Matthew John looked at Annabelle Sue.

Annabelle Sue raised her eyebrows. 'Show yourselves, you bad bats!' she commanded.

Four big ugly bat faces peeped at them over a parapet of ice.

'What are your names?' asked Joshua Ryan.

'Medium Bad Bat,' said the first.

'Small Bad Bat,' said the second.

'Wimpy Bad Bat,' said the third.

'Mad Bad Bat,' said the fourth.

146

'They must be four crew members from Big Bad Bat's black ship,' said Joshua Ryan quietly.

'Marooned here when the black ship left in a hurry,' said Matthew John, nodding. 'They do sound a bit afraid.' He raised his chin. 'We won't hurt you,' he said.

'It's not you we're worried about,' said Mad Bad Bat. 'It's that howling we hear. Wow-ooo-raa-ah! Wow-ooo-raa-ah!'

'What *makes* that noise?' asked Wimpy Bad Bat. 'We have heard it coming nearer and nearer.'

'You are hearing a hunting pack of wolves,' said Annabelle Sue.

'The wolves have chewed their way inside First Seed,' said Emily Charlotte, 'and are chasing after us. We think they plan to eat us.'

The four ugly bats twittered anxiously among themselves.

'We don't want to be eaten,' said Wimpy Bad Bat at length.

'Nor do we,' said Matthew John. He took a deep breath. 'Let's join forces,' he suggested.

'Work together?' said Wimpy Bad Bat, startled. 'Bats and… people?'

'Why not? Come out from behind that rock, all of you, and stand where we can see you!' said Matthew John.

Hoomp-diddy!   Hoomp-diddy!   Hoomp-diddy! Hoomp-diddy!

The four black bats came bouncing out from hiding, riding on their pogo sticks. They looked very big indeed to Matthew John, who was accustomed to the company of smaller bats.

'We are four bad bats (bounce) who ride (bounce) and bounce (bounce) on our pogo sticks (bounce),' said Small Bad Bat.

'We can use our pogo sticks (bounce) to frighten off the wolves,' (bounce) said Mad Bad Bat hopefully.

'We can bounce (bounce) right over their heads!' (bounce) said Wimpy Bad Bat, trying to convince herself that what she was saying was true.

'We shall awe them (bounce) with fashion and flair (bounce),' said Medium Bad Bat, painting her nails with Petulant-in-Pink, not an easy thing to do when you are bouncing on a pogo stick.

'Ah,' said Matthew John. His time as air commodore of the bat rider squadrons had taught him the importance of being tactful. 'Ah' was a useful thing to say sometimes when you did not want to say anything critical. It seemed to him that these four castaway bats, despite their impressive size, were going to need his help, and were going to need it soon. 'May we teach you to fly?' he proposed boldly.

The four big black bats stopped bouncing and gazed at Matthew John as if seeing him for the first time.

'Whatever do you mean?' said Medium Bad Bat.

'Fly?' said Small Bad Bat, frowning.

'We're not *birds*,' said Wimpy Bad Bat.

'We're bats,' said Mad Bad Bat. 'We ride *pogo sticks*.'

'You *are* bats,' said Joshua Ryan, 'and you *can* fly.

148

You were born to fly. You have wings. Think about it. On your own planet the air may be too thin for flying, but here on our planet the air is thick. Go on! I dare you to flap your wings! See what happens!'

'It's easy when you know how,' said Emily Charlotte, encouragingly. 'But hurry! Here come the wolves.'

Wow-ooo-raa-ah! Wow-ooo-raa-ah!

Loopy the alpha male wolf ran with his family up the spiral ramp inside the tree. He was hot on the scent.

As the leader of the pack, it was Loopy's job to find the bat rider who smelled of Cupcake Frostyboots, but there were all these animals wandering about the ramp. Some had horns. He was amazed. 'Did you ever see the like?' he asked his wife.

'Never,' said Loo, her paws making neat prints in the fresh snow as she ran beside her mate. 'Are we wolves or what?'

'I'm going to bring me down one of them woolly things,' said their son Bonkers.

'First we eat the bat rider,' said Loopy, sternly.

'Bat rider?' said Bonkers. 'Forget about the bat rider. I bet one of them woolly things would taste better than any old bat rider. Just one woolly thing? Please? Bet you can't stop me!'

'Leave the mammoths alone, son,' said Loo, 'and do as your father tells you. Stay focused. Remember, this is a hunt for Cupcake Frostyboots.'

The wolves trotted into a second ice cavern. Here the smell of Cupcake Frostyboots was overpowering. The wolves looked at one another, their eyes shining blue-green.

'Spread out,' said Loopy. 'Make like sheep!'

Trembling with the thrill of the chase, Loopy moved stealthily across the floor of the cave, his belly on the ice. 'Baaa,' he said. 'Baaa.' He was a sheep.

Soon he could see the bat riders and the bats. He could even hear them talking.

'The wolves are coming,' Matthew John was saying to Small Bad Bat, 'but I am afraid you'll never escape from them on pogo sticks. If you do not learn to fly, you will die.'

'What do wolves look like?' asked Small Bad Bat, jumping off his pogo stick, and peering nervously into the far reaches of the cavern.

'Huge furry dogs,' said Emily Charlotte.

'With lots of teeth,' said Annabelle Sue, 'and claws.' She held up her hands, curled her fingers, and pawed at the air. 'Grrr!' she said, pretending to be a

150

wolf.

'The things creeping towards us look more like sheep than dogs,' said Wimpy Bad Bat, unbuckling her false arms and laying them down beside her pogo stick on the ground. She would not need her false arms if she was not going to be using her pogo stick. 'Let's run away.'

'The wolves would just run after you,' said Joshua Ryan.'

'Oh, well,' said Medium Bad Bat, fixing her hair and putting her comb away in a little bag that hung by a leather thong around her neck. 'I suppose we'll have to learn to fly, then.' She flexed her shoulders experimentally. Her wings extended and retracted like umbrellas made of skin stretched over light, thin bones. 'I'm going to miss my false arms.'

'You'll all have to unbuckle your false arms and leave them behind with your pogo sticks,' said Matthew John. 'False arms would only get in your way when you are flying. But don't worry. Each of you will have a rider sitting on your back to help.'

'You want to make us into beasts of burden?' said Wimpy Bad Bat.

'No we don't,' said Matthew John firmly. 'We want to help you escape from the wolves. Put down your false arms and your pogo stick, and I'll climb up on your back, Wimpy. Medium Bad Bat, you can give Emily Charlotte a ride, and Small Bad Bat, would you mind being ridden by Joshua Ryan? You'll find him very sensible. As for you, Mad Bad Bat, I think you might enjoy having Annabelle Sue on your back. She is good company. Everybody ready?'

'They *look* like sheep,' said Small Bad Bat.

'They are wolves. Trust me. They are just trying to fool us,' said Matthew John, and he leapt astride Wimpy Bad Bat's back. 'Flap your wings, Wimpy! Let's go!'

The eight wolves gave up pretending to be sheep, growled savagely and ran towards the bat riders.

Emily Charlotte sprang to Medium Bad Bat's back. 'Stop doing your nails, Medium Bad Bat. Time to take off!'

Joshua Ryan settled himself on Small Bad Bat's back. 'One firm downward sweep of your wings would make a good start,' he said.

Annabelle Sue squeezed Mad Bad Bat with her knees. 'Let's see what you've got, Mad Bad Bat!'

Wow-ooo-raa-ah! The wolves sprang.

The four bats flapped their wings and shot up into the air.

Matthew John bumped his head on the domed ceiling of the ice cavern. He leaned forward and patted his bat's neck. 'Well done, Wimpy! Now keep those wings flat and stiff for a moment and see if you can glide.'

'Like this?' Wimpy swooped over the heads of the wolves and right out of the cavern.

'Perfect,' said Matthew John. 'Are you sure you've never flown before?'

'Never,' said Wimpy. 'How am I doing?'

'You're doing great. Flap your wings some more now, but flap your right wing harder than your left.'

As Wimpy did as she was told, Matthew John risked a quick look back over his shoulder, and saw that his friends had taken to the air and were following him out of the cave. Below them, eight baffled wolves dashed about and bumped into one another. The sudden disappearance of their prey had bewildered them. They had run long and far, only to be cheated out of their meal at the last moment. Matthew John felt sorry for them.

'Head for First Seed's tree garden!' he shouted to his friends, and pointed upward.

Matthew John was happy to be riding a bat again. He had thought his days as a bat rider were over, but here he was back in the air, riding a bat stronger and bigger than any he had known. While he missed his old bat Bulmer with whom he had shared a good many adventures, this new bat, Wimpy, seemed to be a born flyer. This was her first flight, and yet she was carrying him effortlessly to the very top of the oldest and highest Yumi tree on the planet. He knew that every Yumi tree had its garden high up in the sky, for he and his fellow bat riders had visited many such gardens while gathering fruit, but he had to wonder: Would First Seed's garden be different from those of her descendants?

It was! Matthew John hugged himself. First Seed's garden was spectacular. It was a Garden of Gardens. White and purple crocuses sprouted from dark loam. Daffodils nodded their golden heads. Fountains leapt and chortled. There was a shady alcove with sides and a roof formed by climbing plants. Orchids brightened ferny nooks. Matthew John took a deep breath. He smelled Angel's Trumpets and the Breath of Heaven.

He and Wimpy Bad Bat soared under a rose trellis and flew low over a bed of wild strawberries.

'My wings are tired,' said Wimpy, anxiously. 'How do I land?'

'Fly upside down and grab a branch firmly with both feet,' said Matthew John.

'Fly upside down?' said Wimpy Bad Bat, doubtfully. 'Are you sure?'

'It's the best way,' said Matthew John. 'Trust me. Here's an arbor that will do nicely. Flip over when I say. One, two, three, and FLIP!'

Wimpy flipped over. She grabbed a sturdy vine with her feet and hung, swaying like a pendulum. She folded her wings over her chest. 'I did it,' she boasted. 'I flew. And now I've made my first landing. What is that strange creature stalking down the garden path, trailing shiny blue feathers?'

'I think it must be a peacock,' said Matthew John. 'I've never seen one before.'

Matthew John slipped down from Wimpy's back. He tiptoed over to the peacock. He scratched its head.

'Hooow-rrr!' said the peacock, who liked having his head scratched. 'Erch! Erch! Erch!'

Matthew John's friends' bats made their own head-over-heels landings, and soon they, too, were swinging upside-down from the same vine. All four bad bats watched their bat riders play with the peacock.

'Is this truly First Seed's garden?' said Emily Charlotte, looking about her at the topiary and the statues.

'Yes, this is my garden,' answered First Seed, 'and I must thank you for scratching my peacock's head. He does enjoy the attention. I am afraid he is a vain creature.'

The bat riders looked up and saw the face of First Seed looking down at them. Although she was the Oldest of Trees, her cheeks glowed with vitality. Matthew John noticed that her bark was a smooth olive-green flecked with cream, while her gleaming eyes were deep green and wrinkly at the corners.

'What are your names?' she asked.

They gave her their names.

'Did you enjoy your journey through my memories?'

'We enjoyed the trip very much, thank you, but it all went by rather fast,' said Matthew John.

'We were being chased by wolves,' Emily Charlotte explained.

'I liked the exciting bits best,' said Annabelle Sue, 'especially the bit when we were cornered by the wolves in the ice cavern.'

'We had to take to the air and skipped some of your more recent memories,' said Joshua Ryan. 'Can you tell us where these big bats came from? The bats we just taught to fly?'

'All the bats, large and small, were born here on this world of ours,' said First Seed, 'but some of them went to live on a distant planet they called Mormoops. You met their leader.'

'Big Bad Bat?' said Matthew John. 'Yes, we met Big Bad Bat. He came here in his black ship and made threats, so we…' He paused, not sure that he wanted to tell First Seed why Big Bad Bat had left in such a hurry.

'We frightened him off,' said Emily Charlotte.

'We gave him a Big Bad Nightmare,' said Annabelle Sue, grinning from ear to ear.

'He burst into tears and he wanted his Mummy,' said Joshua Ryan.

Matthew John bit his lip. He could not look First Seed in the eye. Instead he watched the peacock pacing about and showing off its gaudy tail. From the world below he heard the faint sound of a bell being struck in the Hall of a Hundred Bats, and the sound reminded Matthew John of the bat rider Akihito Akemi who had saved Annabelle Sue from the big wave that struck Kanji island. Akihito Akemi had been brave.

'A bat rider must be brave, helpful and kind,' Mr. Seeds had said years ago on the day Matthew John had joined Number Five Squadron and had become a bat rider.

Had Matthew John been a *brave* bat rider? He frowned. In a way, maybe he had been brave. Certainly he had entered the dark lair of the leopard of Kanji. He had felt his way forward into that dreadful place, not knowing what or whom he might meet there.

Had he been a *helpful* bat rider? He had helped Mr. Seeds operate on the wounded Yumi tree Boris. He had helped with the building of the new school to replace the one destroyed by the big wave.

Had he been a *kind* bat rider? He was not so sure. He had encouraged Hannah Brianna to learn to ride on Bulmer's back, and he had tried to make Bulmer feel good about having a new bat rider. But had he been kind during the crisis when Big Bad Bat had threatened to cut down the forest with his tree-eating machines? He did not think so.

He lifted his chin and looked up at First Seed. He found that he could not see her clearly. Perhaps it was the altitude that was making his eyes water.

'I was unkind to Big Bad Bat,' he made himself say. 'I should not have shown Big Bad Bat the baby tiger. I should not have frightened him. I should not have reminded him of his worst nightmare. I should not have made him cry.'

'Being kind to an enemy is never easy,' said First Seed, 'but it is the only way to make peace.'

'How may I undo the wrong I have done?' asked Matthew John.

'You may chase after the Black Ship,' said First Seed. 'You may find Big Bad Bat and tell him you are sorry that you upset him. You may see if you can persuade him to return. These things you may do. The truth is that we on this planet have great need of Big Bad Bat and of his people. We don't want our forests destroyed, but we do need help to harvest our fruit. We Yumi trees grow higher every day, and every day our tree gardens rise higher into the sky. Flying up to harvest the fruit in our ever-higher gardens is becoming harder and harder work for the small bats. They are quite out of breath these days. We need bigger bats to help them.'

Matthew John's jaw dropped. 'You want me to bring Big Bad Bat and his followers *back*?'

'You did admit that it was wrong of you to frighten him away,' said First Seed, 'and you did ask me to suggest a way to undo that wrong.'

'Indeed I did,' said Matthew John, scratching an itchy place on his back. He made up his mind. 'Very well,' he said. 'I'll do as you ask, First Seed. I'll find Big Bad Bat and tell him I'm sorry.'

'Do you think you will be able to teach Big Bad Bat to fly?' asked Mr. Seeds, wheeling his chair out of a garden pavilion to join them.

159

'I can try,' said Matthew John.

'The harder you try, the higher you fly, and the more you eat pie,' said Matthew John's father.

'Daddy!' exclaimed Matthew John, looking over his shoulder. 'You're so silly. Whatever are you doing here?'

'The Emperor of the Moths very kindly gave your mother and I a lift in his shuttle.'

'I see you've found yourself a new bat,' said Matthew John's mother, and gave Matthew John a hug. 'Aren't you going to introduce us?'

'Sure,' said Matthew John, wriggling out of his mother's embrace. Parents were so embarrassing. 'Mum, Dad, I want you to meet Wimpy. She's very strong and far bigger than Bulmer. Wimpy, these are my parents.'

'Pleased to meet you, Wimpy,' said Matthew John's father.

'Your son taught me to how to fly and how to land,' said Wimpy Bad Bat. She lowered her voice and added 'He is kinder than he knows.'

Matthew John's mother stroked the fur on top of Wimpy Bad Bat's head. 'What became of your pogo stick and your false arms, Wimpy?' she asked.

'We left them behind when we were attacked by wolves,' said Wimpy.

Matthew John's Mum and Dad looked at one another. 'Wolves?' said his mother faintly. 'Did you say you were attacked by... wolves?'

Wow-ooo-raa-ah! Wow-ooo-raa-ah!

Loopy's wolf pack broke from the shrubbery at the

top of the ramp. They rushed towards Matthew John's parents.

Spinning on his heel, Matthew John reached up over his head and plucked eight ripe Yumi fruit from a branch. He tossed the fruit to his friends and to the four bats. 'Quick,' he said. 'The wolves are hungry. Feed them!' He jammed a Yumi fruit into the mouth of the nearest wolf, who happened to be Bonkers.

Joshua Ryan jammed a Yumi fruit into the mouth of Loopy.

Emily Charlotte jammed a Yumi fruit into the mouth of Loo.

Annabelle Sue and the four bad bats stuffed Yumi fruit into the mouths of the other members of the pack.

The wolves stopped in their tracks.

They gazed at one another, shocked and awed.

Yumi juice trickled down their chins.

'Thith ith deliciouth,' said Bonkers, biting down on the fruit.

'Scrumptiouth,' said Loopy, swallowing.

'Yummy in the tummy,' agreed Loo.

The whole pack was as pleased as could be. They had never tasted anything so good. Yumi fruit was way better than Cupcake Frostyboots. Their long hunt was over. They settled down on their haunches and chewed away at the wonderful fruit that grew in the Garden of Gardens, high in the sky.

Matthew John reached for his Bat Rider phone. 'Artibcus? Prepare all decks for departure.'

'You're leaving already?' said Matthew John's mother, dismayed.

Matthew John frowned. 'I have to, Mum, if we are to catch Big Bad Bat. It's my fault, you see. I frightened Big Bad Bat and made him cry. I shouldn't have done that. So now I must try and find him and comfort him.'

Splash!

Bulmer belly-flopped into First Seed's goldfish pond.

Hannah Brianna leapt from Bulmer's back. She squeezed water from the hem of her yellow dress. 'Bulmer and I have been listening to what you were saying. We want to come with you, Matthew John,' she said, breathlessly. 'Bulmer says you need him to navigate. Say you'll take us. Please?'

'Have you asked your Mum and Dad?' asked Matthew John, trying to make his voice sound as deep and calm as First Seed's.

'We'll allow her to go,' said Hannah Brianna's father, stepping from a rose bower.

'We wish them both a safe journey,' said Hannah Brianna's mother, joining her husband, 'she and that bat of hers who has such trouble with his landings. So far as we are concerned, Hannah Brianna may join your expedition, if you will agree to have her.'

'Come on then, Hannah Brianna,' said Matthew John. 'Let's go!'

'Before you do go, Matthew John,' said Mr. Seeds, 'I have news for you. You are appointed Air Vice-Marshall of the Bat Riders.'

'Me?' said Matthew John. 'Air Vice-Marshall? But I made Big Bad Bat sad. I don't deserve promotion.'

162

'Moments ago, you saved your parents from a pack of hungry wolves,' said Mr. Seeds. 'I was impressed by your quick thinking and by your decisive action.'

'Well done, Air Vice-Marshall Matthew John,' said First Seed, 'and the best of luck. Your ship is waiting.'

164

CHAPTER VI

Bulmer's Birthday Cake

BULMER blows out the candle on his birthday cake. 'It looks wonderful,' he says, licking his lips. 'White Mountain icing. My favorite.'

'Shall I help you cut the cake?' I ask.

'If you wouldn't mind,' says Bulmer.

The cake is shaped like Mount Boom and decorated with cherries. I slice the mountain up carefully, making sure every bat gets a cherry.

'Not bad,' says Pinky, eating her cherry first.

'We had better save a piece for Matthew John,' says Bulmer.

'Good idea. And a piece for Wimpy too.'

'Matthew John made the big bad bat cry,' says Suki.

'But he saved the Yumi trees,' says Crystal.

'Will he meet Big Bad Bat again?' asks Bulmer.

'I wouldn't be surprised,' I say.

'Can we have another story?'

'Not tonight. Listen! I hear Wimpy's wingbeats. Matthew John is coming. Close your eyes, everybody. Pretend you're asleep.'

'We'll surprise him,' says Pinky.

ABOUT THE AUTHOR

Anthony Barton lives on an island. As he writes about Matthew John and Bulmer, he sees little brown bats dart past his window, enjoying the warm evening air, and feeding on insects. The baby bats take four weeks to grow as big as their parents. Anthony Barton has a website where you may find more stories about Matthew John. His website is anthonybarton.com

FREE BAT RIDER SERIAL

An Audio Serial for Boys and Girls
by the Same Author
Anthony Barton

Bat Rider and the Cave of Oomba

Bat Rider and the Cave of Oomba is an eight-part serial.
Narration is by the author, with music, bat squeaks and production by
Siri Arnet. All eight episodes are free and may be heard at iTunes and
Podiobooks.com

NOW AVAILABLE

E-Books for Boys and Girls

The Bat Rider Adventures

Matthew John's adventures may be downloaded to your
mobile device, phone, tablet or e-book reader from Apple,
Barnes and Noble, Sony, Kobo, Diesel, Scrollmotion and
Smashwords.com

www.ingramcontent.com/pod-product-compliance
Lightning Source LLC
Chambersburg PA
CBHW060820120626
46557CB00001B/303